BURNING SEASON

Books by Kiki Swinson

PLAYING DIRTY

NOTORIOUS

WIFEY

I'M STILL WIFEY

LIFE AFTER WIFEY

THE CANDY SHOP

A STICKY SITUATION

STILL WIFEY MATERIAL

STILL CANDY SHOPPING

WIFE EXTRAORDINAIRE

WIFE EXTRAORDINAIRE RETURNS

CHEAPER TO KEEP HER

CHEAPER TO KEEP HER 2

THE SCORE

CHEAPER TO KEEP HER 3

CHEAPER TO KEEP HER 4

THE MARK

CHEAPER TO KEEP HER 5

DEAD ON ARRIVAL

THE BLACK MARKET

THE SAFE HOUSE, BLACK MARKET 2

PROPERTY OF THE STATE, BLACK MARKET 3

THE DEADLINE

PUBLIC ENEMY # 1

PLAYING WITH FIRE

PLAYING THEIR GAMES

BURNING SEASON

KIKI SWINSON

DAFINA

www.kensingtonbooks.com

DAFINA BOOKS are published by

Kensington Publishing Corp.
119 West 40th Street
New York, NY 10018

All Kensington Titles, Imprints, and Distributed Lines are available at special quantity discounts for bulk purchases for sales promotions, premiums, fund-raising, and educational or institutional use. Special book excerpts or customized printings can also be created to fit specific needs. For details, write or phone the office of the Kensington special sales manager: Kensington Publishing Corp., 119 West 40th Street, New York, NY 10018, attn: Special Sales Department, Phone: 1-800-221-2647.

Library of Congress Control Number: 2022950819

The DAFINA logo is a trademark of Kensington Publishing Corp.

ISBN: 978-1-4967-3899-8
First Kensington Hardcover Edition: May 2023

ISBN-13: 978-1-4967-3901-8 (ebook)

10 9 8 7 6 5 4 3 2 1

Printed in the United States of America

BURNING SEASON

PROLOGUE

When Things Went Left

I COULDN'T BELIEVE THAT I WAS SITTING IN THE BANK MANAGER'S OF-fice talking to federal agents about a check I was trying to de-posit into my account, along with money I already had sitting in there. Could I really get locked up for the rest of my life? To hear the words "will spend the rest of your life in federal prison" evoked a different kind of reaction inside me. I'd seen Court TV and the reactions of men and women after they got sentenced to lengthy prison terms. I'd also heard so many horror stories about doing prison time with other inmates that are dangerous and will kill you for a fucking honey bun, or to prove a point, and that wasn't my idea of how I wanted to live out the rest of my life. I wanted to have kids and watch them grow up, go off to col-lege, and have families of their own.

Sitting here in this chair, surrounded by federal officers, was not the ticket. All I had to do was tell them that Alonzo gave me the check, but then where would that leave him? I'd be ratting my brother out and that went against everything that I believed in. I was taught as a child that family stuck together. Never let anyone come between us. Our father embedded that in our family's heads. Zo lived by those same values. So I refused to let any agent come between that.

"Excuse me, Agents. But am I under arrest?"

Both agents looked at one another. And then they turned their attention toward me. "No, you're not," the female federal agent replied.

I stood up and walked toward the door of the bank manager's office.

"You know that if you walk out of here, there's no coming back," the female federal agent commented.

"Say no more," I told her, and then exited the office. The agents watched as the door closed shut.

CHAPTER 1

Alayna

I WAS ON THE PHONE TALKING WHEN LEVI ENTERED OUR BEDROOM. "I'm gonna call you back," I told the caller, and then ended the call. This pissed Levi off.

"Who was that? And why did you end the call when I walked into the bedroom?"

"I didn't end the call because you walked in. I was going to end it anyway."

"It must've been your side piece."

"What side piece? Trust me, you're all the man I can handle at once," I said, trying to assure him. But he wasn't buying it. Levi knows that things have changed in our marriage. We have sex less and I don't spend time with him like I used to. And this bothered him. I mean, if the shoe was on the other foot, it would bother me too.

"Come on, let's get out of here. I've gotta get to work," he mentioned, and left the bedroom.

He was sitting inside my car when I exited the house. He and I had been carpooling for the past week because his 2017 Dodge Charger was in the shop getting a new transmission. My 2021 Jeep Wrangler was his source of transportation for the moment and he hated it, especially when he had to drop me off at work in front of Tim and my brother, Alonzo.

All eyes were on us when we pulled up in the parking lot. Tim, Alonzo, Jesse, and the volunteer Paul were sitting on the picnic table that the firemen use to congregate and shoot the breeze when we're not cleaning the fire station or one of the trucks.

As soon as Levi stopped the Jeep, I gave him a quick peck on the lips and then climbed out of it. "What kind of kiss was that?"

"What do you mean 'what kind of kiss was that?' It was a kiss."

"I see what you're doing?"

"What are you talking about?" I asked while standing next to the passenger-side door.

"You tried to hurry up and kiss me so your boyfriend wouldn't see you," Levi said as he watched my brother, Alonzo, approach my Jeep.

"What's going on, family?" Alonzo asked after he came within arm's distance of us.

"Everything is all good." Levi spoke first.

Alonzo turned his attention towards me. "Ready to work?" Alonzo asked me.

"As always," I replied.

"Do you know what you're trying to cook tonight?" Alonzo reminded me.

"Oh, yeah. I forgot."

"We're all gonna pile into the truck and head to the store in about thirty minutes. So put a list together," he encouraged me.

"Will do," I said, and walked away from the Jeep.

"You ain't gonna say goodbye to your man?" Alonzo blurted out.

"I kissed him earlier," I said without looking back.

"She's trying to hurry up and get over there to her boyfriend," Levi commented.

Alonzo burst into laughter. "Who? Tim?"

"Yeah, her sugar daddy."

I pretended not to hear him say that.

"Oh, nah, ain't nothing going on with those two," I heard my brother say.

"Alonzo, don't blow smoke up my ass. I know what I see."

"Well, if you think you see something, then I'm not gonna argue with you."

"I appreciate it," Levi said, and then sped off.

Me and Tim watched as Levi sped away in my Jeep.

"Looks like someone is upset," Tim commented.

"He's just being a jerk," I replied.

"He thinks you two are having a fling," Alonzo mentioned.

Tim and I both looked at one another and then we looked at Alonzo.

"What gave him that impression?" Tim asked Alonzo.

"He didn't say," Alonzo answered.

"I told him that he needs to stop being so insecure," I added.

"What made him suspect something was going on between you guys in the first place?"

"He complains about Tim texting me too much."

"He's your boss," Alonzo interjected.

"I told him that," I said.

"Did you tell Alonzo that he called me the night before, asking where you were?" Tim chimed in.

"No," I replied.

"While you were here at work?" Alonzo asked, wanting clarity.

"Yeah. I had just washed the dishes in the kitchen."

"And I was helping him."

"Where was I?" Alonzo wanted to know.

"I think you and Jesse was outside cleaning up the truck by then," I answered.

"I wonder why he didn't call me?" Alonzo asked us.

"He's still salty about how you screamed at him during the NBA Finals and never paid the bet you owed him," I explained.

"No way. He still thinks I owe him?"

"Yep. He bet on the Bucks winning. And your money was on the Phoenix Suns."

"Yeah, but the Bucks was supposed to beat the Suns by ten points. But they only got them by seven."

I chuckled. "He said that was bullshit and that you threw that ten point–game clause in there when the game was almost over."

Tim chuckled. "That sounds like you, Alonzo."

"No. I added that during halftime."

"Alonzo, just pay him the money," I insisted.

"I don't even remember how much the bet was."

"One hundred dollars," I reminded him.

"One hundred dollars?" Tim interjected. "Oh, Levi can forget it. This cheap motherfucker here isn't going to give anyone one hundred dollars."

"Yeah, I don't remember it being that much," Alonzo added.

I let out a long sigh. "Alonzo, just give Levi the money. He won it fair and square."

"I'm not giving him one hundred bucks. Maybe twenty." Alonzo flat out refused.

"Why don't you give him fifty instead?" Tim suggested.

"Yeah, that would be a nice gesture. Meet him in the middle," I agreed.

"I'm not giving up one hundred or fifty. Twenty-five dollars is my final offer."

I threw my hands up in the air. "Getting money out of Alonzo is like pulling teeth," I commented, and then walked off and headed into the fire station. Jesse and Paul followed me.

"Don't get mad because I know how to hold on to my money!" he yelled behind me.

I ignored him and continued into the building, leaving them two out there alone. Hanging out at the fire station was my passion. I lived for this place, and it didn't hurt that I had a little love thing going on with Tim while I was here. This would kill Levi. But I figured what he didn't know wouldn't hurt him.

CHAPTER 2

Alonzo

"**R**EMIND ME NEVER TO BET AGAINST YOU ON ANYTHING," TIM commented, and then he chuckled.

Before I could respond, my cellular phone started ringing, so I retrieved the phone from his side pocket and looked at the caller ID. It was my fiancée, Pricilla Gates. I met Pricilla at a sports bar. I was there with a couple of high school buddies watching the play-offs and introduced myself. We talked and hit it off, and fast-forward three years later, we're still together. Just seven months ago, I proposed to her and she said yes, so we're now planning a wedding. Hopefully, kids will follow.

"Hey, future Mrs. Riddick, how can I help you?" I started off the conversation, and put her on speakerphone.

"I'm good, baby. I was calling to remind you that we have a cake tasting on Friday. That's the day you get off, so don't take on an extra day there at the station."

I started laughing.

"Don't laugh. I'm serious. You tried that stunt before and I had to reschedule."

"Pricilla, I'm gonna make sure he makes that appointment," Tim interjected.

"Is that Tim?"

"Yes, it's me."

"How are you?"

"I'm great, and you?"

"I'm good. And, yes, please make sure he doesn't try to stay there after his shift is over Friday morning."

"I will, and you have my word," Tim assured her.

"Thank you, Tim. Okay, baby, you there?"

"Yes, I'm here."

"I'm gonna go now. I love you."

"I love you too," I told her, and then ended the call.

"Sounds like you're dragging your feet. You're not having second thoughts, are you?"

"Oh, no, I've just been busy, trying to get this money. I told her to go and do the cake tasting with her mother and her sister. But, no, she wants me there for some reason. I couldn't care less about all the flavors we could choose from. Just give me a yellow cake with vanilla icing and I'm fine."

"Boy, don't I remember those times. I was just like you. I told my wife to go and take care of everything and I'll just meet her at the altar. And guess what she did?"

"What?"

"She grabbed me by my ear and dragged me to the venue, the floral shop, the tuxedo place, the catering place, and the bakery that made our cake. The only place I didn't go was to the bridal shop when she picked out her gown. And, boy, was I happy."

I chuckled. "You're a funny dude, Tim."

"So, how much has this wedding set you back thus far?"

"Our initial budget was fifty thousand. But by the time this is over, I'm gonna probably fork out one hundred thousand."

"Wow! That's a lot of money. Do you know my wedding only cost us ten thousand?"

"That was what? Over 15 years ago?"

"It was. . . ."

Before Tim could finish his sentence, my cell phone started ringing again. I looked at the caller ID. "This is the call we've been waiting for," I told him, and answered the call.

"Hello," I said.

"The check cleared this morning," Amy started off saying.

"That was quick," I replied with enthusiasm.

"We knew it wasn't gonna take long."

"So, did you withdraw some cash?" I got quick to the point.

"Yes, we did."

"Did you get what we asked you?"

"Yes."

"All right. Sounds good. Could you meet me at the Harris Teeter grocery store in about forty-five minutes?"

"Yes."

"Okay, great. See you then," I said cheerfully, and disconnected the call. "That was Amy. The couple that lives on Lancaster."

"Yeah."

"Their check cleared this morning. We have eight thousand coming our way."

"I thought we agreed to get twenty-five grand on that one."

"We did. Remember, they gave us eight a month after the fire? They are giving us eight more today. And then I'm going to have them give us the last nine next week."

"Oh, okay, I remember now," Tim said.

"Has the old guy from Lake Edward called you back yet?"

"Last time I talked to him, he said that he was still waiting on his check."

"Hasn't it been over four months now?" Tim seemed worried.

"Yeah, and something's telling me that he already got the check and is holding out on us."

"You might wanna give him a call."

"Why don't we just stop by there later tonight?"

"Let's do that," I agreed, and then we dapped each other a handshake and headed into the fire station.

I drove the fire truck to the grocery store, while Tim, my sister, Alayna, our other firefighter, Jesse, and a volunteer named Paul sat in the other sections of the truck. As soon as the truck stopped, everyone climbed out. "Hey, Alayna, you got the grocery list?" I asked her as we all headed across the parking lot.

"Yep, I sure do."

"All right, well, I'm gonna meet y'all inside," I announced as I made a detour in another direction of the parking lot. Tim knew where I was going and gave me a head nod.

I searched the parking lot for Amy's car and finally saw it parked eleven cars away. She and her husband, Mitch, were sitting in the car, waiting for me, as I approached it. I smiled as I walked toward them. And as soon as I got within a few feet of the driver's-side door, I greeted the husband first, because he was the driver.

"How are you doing?" I asked and extended a handshake.

"I'm good, and you?" Mitch replied, and shook my hand.

I leaned over into the driver's-side window and spoke to Amy, who was sitting on the passenger side of the car. "How are you over there?"

She smiled. "I'm great. Beautiful day out."

"I can't agree more."

The husband held a white envelope toward the window and I reached over and grabbed it. "This is the second installment you asked us for. You'll get the other nine next week."

I took the envelope and pushed it down in my front right pocket. "Thank you very much," I said. "Have you guys started the repairs yet?" I asked, making idle conversation. It would've been rude to take the money and just leave.

"We've got a contractor working on it as we speak," Mitch said.

"Did they say how long it's gonna take?" I wondered aloud.

"The back porch will take a week. The back bedroom will take ten days," he answered.

"That's not too bad," I replied.

"I think we could've gotten it done sooner. But Mitch wants to be cheap and this crew doesn't work fast," Amy interjected.

"Hold up, little lady. There is nothing wrong with being cheap," I commented, and laughed.

"I keep telling her, saving a buck here and there will go a long way," Mitch announced.

"I agree with you one hundred percent," I said, and then smiled at them both. I looked down at my watch purposely, so I could give them a reason that I had to run off. "I could do this all day, folks. But I'm gonna have to run in this grocery store and get a few things for the fire station."

"Oh, well, don't let us hold you. Take care of your business and we'll call you next week," Mitch insisted.

"Sounds good. Talk to you folks then," I replied, tapped on the hood of their car, and then walked off.

The moment I entered the grocery store, I searched the aisle for Tim. I finally found him near the deli department. "I got the money."

"Were they acting nervous like they did the first time?"

"No, they were acting pretty calm this time."

"Did you count it?"

"No. I just stuck it in my pocket and came in here."

"Come on, let's go in the men's bathroom and count it," Tim instructed me. "I'll be right back," he told the deli worker, and then walked off. I followed in his footsteps. As soon as we entered the bathroom, I made sure that we were there alone. And when I realized that we were by ourselves, I took the money out of the envelope and began to count. When I got to the end, I noticed that we were short five hundred dollars. This pissed Tim off. "Get on the phone and call their ass now." I could almost see steam coming from his ears as he watched me dial the phone number.

"Hello," I said immediately after Amy answered the phone.

"Yes?"

"You know you guys shorted us five hundred dollars?" I informed her. She fell silent. "Hello," I said once again.

"Yeah, I'm here."

"Did you hear what I said?"

"You said it was short?" she asked.

"Yes, five hundred."

"Hello," I heard her husband's voice say.

"Hey, Mitch, we're short five hundred dollars."

"Are you sure? I counted it myself. I was sure I put eight thousand in the envelope."

"There's only seventy-five hundred in here."

"I'm sorry about that. Can I add it to next week's final payment?"

Livid from his question, I put them on mute and folded my phone into the palm of my hand. "He asked if he could add the other five hundred to the last installment for next week?" I asked Tim.

Tim looked like he wanted to punch the wall. But he remained calm and said okay after waiting about five seconds.

"Yeah, Mitch, next week is fine. But make sure it's ninety-five hundred instead of nine thousand," I told him.

"Will do," he said, and then the phone went dead. I placed the phone back inside my pocket and looked at Tim.

"He's full of shit and he knows it," Tim hissed. He was seething.

"Look, we'll take three thousand seven hundred fifty each. And look at it like this, after next week, we don't have to deal with him anymore."

Tim took his portion of the money and handed me the envelope with the rest. I shoved it down into my pocket and gave him a pat on the back. "It's not the end of the world," I commented, and then exited the bathroom. He followed a couple of seconds later.

Back in the store, I found Alayna with a basket full of groceries and a list of items that she still needed to get. So I helped her. During out trip down the bread aisle, we began to reminisce about our father and his contribution as the city's fire chief before his untimely death. "Pop was the best fire chief this city has ever seen," I started off saying. "Everyone, from the community leaders to the citizens, loved him."

"I know," she said, and smiled proudly.

"Do you know about all the food drives he used to organize?"

"Of course, I do. He had us both there and volunteering."

"What about the toy drives! It was his mission to make sure every child in the city of Virginia Beach have a toy under their Christmas tree."

"Do you remember when he invited those homeless people to our house on Thanksgiving that one time?" Alayna reminded me.

I smiled. "Yeah, I remember that. Mom wasn't too happy about it."

"He's the real reason why I joined the fire department, and for lots of other recruits too," Alayna admitted.

"Absolutely. He was my reason for signing up too. Our dad was a good man."

"Yep. He sure was," Alayna agreed.

"What are you two youngsters talking about?" Tim asked as he approached us.

"My dad," Alayna answered in a boastful way.

"Oh, Chief Riddick. The most respected man in the city of Virginia Beach," Tim acknowledged.

"Yeah, he was your boss too."

"Yes, and sometimes a pain in my ass," Tim commented, and then he chuckled. "He meant well though. He was definitely a good man. And he taught me everything I know."

"He taught us all," I added.

"I wish he was here now," Alayna said aloud.

"If he was, he would be so proud of you," Tim insisted.

"I tell her that all the time," I agreed.

"Got enough food in that grocery cart?" a cop, who came out of nowhere, asked. He was a white cop dressed in uniform. Tim chuckled loudly and started walking toward the cop, and that's when I knew that they knew each other. Alayna and I looked at one another and hunched our shoulders.

"What's going on, buddy? Haven't seen you in ages," Tim told the cop after he embraced him and patted him on his back.

"It's been, what, fifteen years or more?" the cop asked.

"Yep, more like twenty years," Tim corrected him.

"I married my college sweetheart. Relocated to Florida, where she was from, and after thirteen years of that, we grew apart, got a divorce, and I came back here."

"How long have you been back in Virginia?"

"Four years."

After a few words into their conversation, Tim realized that he hadn't introduced Bobby, his cop friend, to Alayna and me, so he turned his attention toward us. He introduced me first and then Alayna. We both smiled, shook his hand, and then they carried on. We excused ourselves to continue shopping, while they continued to catch up.

"Sounds like they've been knowing each other for a long time," Alayna mentioned as we pushed the grocery cart away from them.

"Somehow I'm getting a weird feeling that he didn't just bump into him. It almost feels like he knew we were all standing on that aisle before he walked onto it."

"You think he was watching us?"

"It wouldn't surprise me if he was."

Alayna chuckled. "You're paranoid. Let's go and finish shopping."

CHAPTER 3

Tim

AFTER CATCHING UP WITH MY OLD FRIEND BOBBY, I MET BACK UP with the crew in the parking lot of the grocery store as they headed toward the fire truck.

"Get everything on the list?" I asked Alayna.

"Yep," she replied as she pushed the cart in the direction of the truck.

"Have we decided on tonight's dinner?" I asked her.

"Yes, we're having spaghetti."

"And I'm cooking it," Alonzo blurted out.

"I thought I was cooking tonight," one of the other firemen interjected from a few feet away.

"I thought so too," I agreed.

"So, wait, no one likes my cooking now?" Alonzo questioned the group in a joking manner.

"What are you talking about? We love your cooking," Alayna commented.

"Doesn't sound that way to me," Alonzo answered.

"Remember, you got fieldwork tonight," I reminded him. He needed to make a trip to the old man's house so we could get the rest of our money from the insurance payout.

"Oh, yeah. Almost forgot about that," he said after I jogged his memory. It's always been my job to keep Alonzo on point. Every so often, he'll veer off track.

Immediately after we arrived at the fire truck, everyone grabbed a grocery bag and piled them into the back storage compartments. When all the bags were packed inside, Alonzo closed the hatch and we all climbed inside and headed back to the fire station.

As soon as we got back to the station, we carried the bags into the kitchen and Alayna sparked up a conversation about Bobby. "Looks like you found your long-lost friend."

"Bobby?"

"Yeah, he seemed happy to see you."

"Yeah, we used to fish together back in the day. Real decent guy. Would give you the shirt off his back."

"Alonzo seems nervous about him."

I chuckled. "For what? Bobby is harmless."

"If he's so harmless, think he'd turn you in if he knew about the payouts?"

"I wouldn't give him a chance to do it."

"What do you mean by that?"

"I wouldn't tell him."

"But what if he could potentially get other people to get in on the action?"

"I wouldn't risk it."

"Okay, sounds good to me."

"So, how you know Alonzo isn't feeling him?"

"Because he told me after we walked away from you guys."

"Did he say anything else?"

"Nope. He just said that he didn't trust him. That's all."

"Well, I'll remind him later that our business dealings are strictly among us. No other outsiders."

"Good. Then it's settled."

"Wanna go to my office for a quickie?"

"Thought you'd never ask," she commented, and then we walked to my office together. Immediately after I closed the door to my office, I reached in my pocket, grabbed the stack of money Alonzo gave me, peeled off two thousand, and handed it to her. Her eyes lit up like she was a kid in a candy store.

"Awww, thank you, baby. I'm gonna put this with the rest of it," she told me.

"You're welcome. Now put it away," I instructed her.

She started stuffing it down in her pants pockets, and as soon as she was done, I grabbed her into my arms and started kissing her on her mouth and around her neck. "I've been wanting to do this ever since you came to work," I said between kisses.

She seemed intoxicated by my sensual kisses and the words coming from my mouth, but she managed to agree with my sentiments. "You have no idea how bad I wanted you too," she said as she wrapped her arms around my neck. This position allowed me to pull her closer into me. When my groin met her pelvic area, I began to grind against her and my dick got hard instantly. Alayna felt it too.

"I got you pretty aroused," she said.

"You feel it too?" I asked her, even though it was a rhetorical question.

She released one of her arms from my neck, slid her hand down my chest, and then to my groin area. She immediately started massaging my erection through my pants. The touch of her hand pushed me to a full erection.

"You're charting dangerous territory," I said between kisses.

"I'm a big girl. I can handle you," she said as she continued to rub her hand against my protruding penis.

"Turn around," I instructed her.

I released her from my arms and turned her around. She now faced my desk. Seconds later, I pushed her in that direction. She walked willingly as I guided her. When we reached my desk, I instructed her to place her hands on top of it and then told her to relax. She did what she was told and allowed me to take over. I began to pull down her pants slowly, revealing a pair of silk black panties. The anticipation of fucking her mounted. The erection in my pants proved it.

"You're gonna fuck me from the back?" she whispered seductively as she looked over her right shoulder.

"Is that how you want it?" I asked her.

Before she could answer, three sudden knocks hit my office door. Startled by the unexpected, Alayna turned around toward me and began to pull up her pants. I stood there, pondering whether or not to ask who it was.

"What are you doing? Say something," Alayna instructed me after she stuffed her shirt back in her pants and zipped up her pants.

"Who is it?" I asked reluctantly.

"It's your wife."

Alayna looked at me in horror. I could tell that she didn't want me to open the door. But I had to, because my wife wasn't going to go anywhere until I did.

"As soon as she sees my face, she's gonna know that we were in here doing something," Alayna whispered.

"Just have a seat. Grab that file on my desk and act like you're reading it," I told her.

While Alayna grabbed the file from my desk, I walked slowly to my office door and then unlocked it.

"What's going on? And why was your door locked?" Kirsten asked me as she pushed her way into my office. A lot of people say that white women are passive and docile. But not my wife. Kirsten looked like a dumb blonde, but she wasn't stupid by a long shot, and if someone pissed her off, she would go off like a firecracker.

"My door wasn't locked," I lied.

"And what is she doing in here?" Kirsten asked as she made her way around me.

Alayna looked up from the file she had in her hand. "And hello to you too," Alayna greeted Kirsten sarcastically.

"But I didn't say hello to you," Kirsten pointed out as she walked toward Alayna's chair.

"I know," Alayna replied, and then she turned her attention back toward the file.

"So, Tim, are you going to tell me why she's in your office while the door is locked?" Kirsten asked after she turned her attention back toward me. By this time, I had closed the door to my office and walked back over to my desk.

"The door wasn't locked, Kirsten." I held tightly on to my lie.

"Tim, please don't play games with me. I know y'all were in here doing something you weren't supposed to do, being that you're a married man," Kirsten observed.

"I see where this is going, so I am going to remove myself from the equation." Alayna spoke up, stood up from her chair, placed the file on my desk, and then proceeded to leave. But Kirsten stepped in front of her, blocking her from leaving my office.

"Where do you think you're going?" Kirsten asked her.

"Where I go is none of your business. Now please get out of my way," Alayna told her.

"And what are you going to do if I don't?" Kirsten continued.

Seeing what was about to go down, I got up from my chair and rushed around my desk to prevent both ladies from having a physical altercation.

Alayna chuckled and then turned her attention toward me. "You better come and get your wife before I—" Alayna began to say, but Kirsten cut her off in midsentence.

"Before you do what? Beat my ass?" Kirsten questioned her as she got in her face.

"Yeah, before I beat your ass!" Alayna snapped, getting back into Kirsten's face.

And in slow motion, I saw Kirsten raise both of her hands with the intent to shove Alayna back from her, but I leaped between them both and pushed Kirsten backward. "Kirsten, you know better than this. Stop it," I scolded her. But my words fell on deaf ears.

"So you're going to take up for her?"

"Kirsten, you started it!" I roared.

Alayna managed to get around Kirsten and me and exited my office. While Alayna was leaving, Alonzo appeared. He approached Alayna.

"What's going on?" he asked.

"Tim's wife is in his office acting like a crazy bitch!" I heard Alayna say. Kirsten heard it too and rushed over to the entryway of my office door.

"What did you just say?" Kirsten roared as she stood before Alonzo and Alayna.

I grabbed her by the arm and yanked her back. "Kirsten, now that is enough."

Kirsten stumbled, trying to watch her step. "She's a home-wrecker and I won't let her tear my family apart!" she shouted.

"Alonzo, would you please take Alayna somewhere while I talk to my wife?" I instructed Alonzo.

"Yeah, sure," Alonzo replied, and walked away from the office door.

Kirsten broke away from my grip and ran down the hallway toward Alonzo and Alayna. "No, you're not going anywhere until you tell me to my face that you're not fucking my husband," she shouted once again. She was making a pure fool out of herself and embarrassing me while she was doing it. I was the freaking chief of the station and I had a certain standard I had to uphold, and with my wife's behavior, she was making it impossible for me to do it.

Once again, I found myself running down behind Kirsten, and when I got within arm's distance of her, I grabbed her by the arm and yanked her backward again. "That's it. You're going home right now," I insisted, and escorted her by the arm as I led her to the front exit of the fire station. She resisted a little, but her strength was no match for mine.

"I know you're fucking my husband, bitch! And it will come out one of these days." She hurled obscenities at Alayna, who was standing with her back against the wall, alongside Alonzo. Alonzo looked like he was in shock.

Alonzo and Alayna watched my wife's fit of rage until we disappeared on the other side of the exit door. Outside, I ripped my wife a new asshole.

"What the fuck is wrong with you? Do you know how embarrassed you just made me?"

"Fuck all of that. Are you fucking her?"

"No, Kirsten, I'm not," I lied.

Did she think that I would admit to doing something like that? Was she on drugs? What man admits to his wife that he's sleeping around on her? Not anyone I know.

"Then what's going on with you two? We don't have sex anymore, like we used to, so you're getting it from somewhere other than home." She stared me down. She was not backing off me.

"Believe me, I'm not having an affair with her."

"Then who are you fucking, Tim? Because you're not getting it from me. Trust me, I noticed a lot of shit has changed around the house and it stops today," she threatened me.

"Okay, I'll have more sex with you."

"But that's not it, Tim. I shouldn't say that to you, and all you say is that you'll have 'more sex' with me. I want you to want me. That's what a couple does, Tim."

"It's only because of stress on the job, honey."

"Then why was your office door locked? And what were you doing in there?" she wanted to know.

"The door wasn't locked." I lied once again.

"Tim, don't play games with me. It was locked. I tried to open it twice and the doorknob wouldn't turn."

"That's because it must've been stuck."

Kirsten stood there and searched my face to see if I was lying to her. In the past, she had the ability to catch me in a few lies. But today I wasn't going to let that happen. "Are you having an affair with her?" She wouldn't let it up.

"No, I am not."

"I don't believe that, Tim. You don't even look at me like you used to. You've changed."

"That's only because working these long hours has gotten the best of me. That's all."

"Tim, we've been married for over fifteen years. I know how your body works. So feed that bullshit to someone else," she said as she folded both of her arms against her chest.

"Look, you're just gonna have to trust what I'm telling you. I'm not having an affair with Alayna, and that's it. End of story."

Kirsten chuckled. "Yeah, okay. You can say 'end of story' now. But if I found out that you're fucking that Black bitch in there, I will destroy your ass. I will divorce you and then I'm going to make sure that you never work in another city position again. You got that?"

See, I knew what she meant by saying that she would destroy me. She knew about my arson kickback payoffs I get from families that file insurance claims. So, in essence, she was saying that if she found out that I was sleeping with Alayna, she would rat me out to the cops. I would get fired and perhaps go to jail. That would definitely ruin me. So I was going to have to keep my nose clean, because I didn't need the heat. Right now, Kirsten held the cards, so I was gonna have to be extra careful from this day forward. My life and freedom depended on it.

"Please don't come back up here with that drama anymore," I told her in a firm tone.

"Don't let me find your office door locked and her inside when I walk through the door."

Ignoring her counter, I said, "To hell with that! You heard what I said. Don't come back up with that drama anymore, or I'm gonna have to stop you from coming up here."

"Yeah, whatever. And you heard what I said too."

I shook my head with frustration. "What did you come up here for anyway?" I wanted to know.

"I came up here to see you, because I was in the area. Is there a crime against that?"

"No, there isn't. But could you call first the next?"

"Fuck no! Have I ever had to call you before? Now see, I know there's something going on. You're changing."

I chuckled. "I am not changing, Kirsten."

"So you think it's funny?"

"No, I don't. Will you please stop it? You're burning me out right now with all of these crazy questions and false assumptions."

"Let me tell you something, a woman knows when her husband is cheating. And you, my dear, are having an affair. I can smell it on you. But I'm warning you, don't let me find out, because if I do, I'm going to end your life."

"So you're threatening to kill me now?"

"Try me and you'll see," she said, and then she turned around and walked away. I watched her as she got into her car and drove away. The way she pulled out of the parking lot, I knew she was furious with me and this wouldn't be the last time she confronted me with this situation. Now I had to go and apologize to Alayna for the way my wife attacked her.

CHAPTER 4

Alayna

ALONZO AND I WALKED INTO THE LOUNGE AREA SO I COULD wind down from the confrontation I had just had with Tim's wife. No one was in the lounge area, but us, so this gave us a chance to speak freely about what had just happened.

"What was that all about?" he started off questioning me, after I sat down on the sectional. He sat down next to me.

"Tim and I was in his office talking, with the door closed. She knocked on the door, Tim let her in, and when she walked in and saw me, she thought that he and I was doing something."

"Doing what?"

"Come on, Zo, you heard her. She thinks that I'm fucking Tim," I said defensively.

"But why would she think that? I don't get it. Were y'all looking suspicious or something when she walked in?"

"I was sitting in one of his chairs looking at a file."

"You know your husband also suspect that you're seeing Tim behind his back?"

"Yeah, I know. He's accused me a few times about it."

"Are you?"

I sucked my teeth. "Of course not, he's my boss."

"Yeah, and you have a husband and Tim has a wife. That

wouldn't be a good look around here. We can't have that type of drama circulating. We're here to work and watch each other's back."

"I know that. And please don't talk to me like I'm a little kid."

"I'm just only giving you the facts."

Seconds later, the door to the lounge area opened and Tim entered. "Are you all right?" he asked as he approached me.

"Yes, I'm good. Is your crazy wife all right?" I asked sarcastically.

"I'm sorry about that. I told her, if she ever did that again, she would be banned from coming here. So I promise that it won't happen again."

"I was just telling Alayna that Levi thinks you two are having an affair too."

"And what did you tell 'em?" Tim asked Zo.

"I laughed it off and told him that it was impossible. And that he had nothing to worry about. Did I tell him something wrong?"

"Oh, no. That was a good answer," Tim replied.

Alonzo looked at me, and then he looked back at Tim, giving off an expression of uncertainty. "Give it to me straight, you guys, are y'all seeing each other?" he asked.

Tim spoke first. "Come on now, Zo, you know me better than that. Alayna is in her twenties. She's like a baby sister to me."

So Alonzo turned his attention toward me. "Is he telling me the truth?" he pressed.

"Yeah, he's telling you the truth. I told you that we weren't sleeping around."

Alonzo stood up from the sofa. "Okay, well, I guess that solves that. You aren't messing around behind your spouses' backs, so we're good here," he said, and then he headed toward the door of the lounge.

"You wanna go take that trip and handle that business now?" Tim suggested.

"Now?" Alonzo wanted clarity.

"Yes, now. The sun is going down, and by the time you get that, it would be dark out," Tim pointed out.

"Yeah, sure. I'll take care of that now," Alonzo assured him, and then made his exit.

After Alonzo closed the door to the lounge area, Tim took a seat next to me. "We're gonna have to stop seeing each other."

Crushed by his words, I looked into his eyes. "But why?"

"Because it's time. Kirsten says that if she finds out that I'm sleeping with you behind her back, she's going to ruin me. Get me fired, and I can't have that."

"But she won't find out. All we have to do is be extra careful." I began to plead with him. Make him see it from my perspective.

"I wish it was that simple."

"But it is. You just gotta see it my way," I told him as I cradled his face with both of my hands.

He took my hands from his face. "Let's just chill for right now. Maybe later, we could rekindle this thing."

"But I don't want to, Tim. I won't be able to walk around here and work alongside you if I can't touch you or be romantically involved with you. That's torture."

"I'm sorry, Alayna, but that's just how things gotta be right now. I've got too much stuff to lose. And besides, it's not just my wife who suspects that we are sleeping around. You heard Alonzo, even your husband sees it."

"Fuck him. He doesn't count. I'm not in love with him anymore. I'm in love with you."

"And I love you too. But we've gotta end this. And we've gotta end this now, before it gets ugly," Tim said adamantly. His words were final.

"So that's it? I have no say-so in this matter?" I asked him as he stood up from the sofa.

"Yes, Alayna, this is it."

Heartbroken, I just sat there and watched Tim as he left me sitting in the lounge room. I wanted to scream to the top of my voice and air out all of our dirty laundry, but then I decided against it. The firefighters that are on call tonight would find out what Tim and I was doing behind closed doors, and then word would get back to the mayor. That's a whole scandal in itself. Tim would lose his job, his pension, and God knows what else. I would definitely lose my job. And who knows, maybe tarnish my father's legacy. I couldn't have that. My brother would be furious with me.

I guess there was nothing I could do but take what happened and deal with it. But then again, how could I work alongside that man, knowing that I couldn't be intimate with him anymore? That was gonna be hard. Maybe I should take off a week or so? Get away from him so that I could collect my thoughts and figure out a way to deal with them?

After I gathered my thoughts and calmed down, I walked out of the lounge area and went into the dining hall. That was where I heard all the talking and commotion. When I entered the room, I saw Tim and a few of our colleagues watching a NASCAR race on TV. They were into it. And they were loud, so I excused myself. To keep myself busy, and not think about Tim breaking up with me, I went outside into the fire truck port and started rearranging all the supplies we use on a daily basis. This solution worked for the first twenty minutes, but when Tim walked into the truck port, he tried his best to act like he hadn't just broken up with me. This annoyed the hell out of me.

"Hey, there you go," he started off. "Thought you disappeared on me."

"Nope. I'm right out here keeping myself busy."

"Need any help?"

"Nope. I've got it. Thank you."

"Dinner is almost ready."

"Great. I'll be in there in a second."

"You better, because you don't want it to get cold."

Becoming increasingly annoyed by his voice, I stopped what I was doing and turned around and faced him. "Will you please leave me alone right now! I'm trying to organize this supply closet and you're badgering me. Please give me some space."

Tim threw his hands up in the air. "My bad. I was only trying to make conversation."

"But you've said enough earlier. So please leave me be."

"As you wish," he said, and then left.

"Fucking loser!" I said, and then slammed a bottle of cleaner onto the floor.

CHAPTER 5

Alonzo

I DIDN'T REALIZE IT AT FIRST, BUT I HAD TWO PICKUPS TONIGHT. ONE from a young guy named Percy. And the other one from Mr. Cole. They didn't live too far apart, so I stopped off at Percy's house first.

Percy Flemings was his name. He was a college kid paying his way through school. I believe he told me that he was twenty-one years old. Either way, the kid had a good head on his shoulders. When I knocked on his door, he didn't hesitate to let me in. When I entered his place, I saw that he had company. A young female companion sat on the couch, watching TV, so I didn't want to stick around there for as long as I had to. Having too many people in your business isn't a good thing to do. After he let me in, he excused himself and returned to the door with a piece of white paper. He held it so tightly in his hand, it made me feel good to know that he and I were on the same page. The less another person knew about our dealings, the better the deal, and everyone won.

"See you got company," I mentioned.

"Yeah, she's my girlfriend."

I asked him to come outside with me. "She doesn't know about this, right?" I asked him after we walked outside.

"Not so much. But don't worry. She's cool."

"Are you sure?"

"Yeah, she's good."

"Okay. Well, don't mention how much money you gave me."

"I wouldn't tell her that."

"Okay. Cool. Well, take care."

"So we're good? My debt is paid?"

"Yeah, you're in the clear."

"Cool," Percy said, and then went back into his house.

I climbed back in my car and started counting the money he had just handed me. It was all there. Five thousand dollars. Tim and I split it down the middle. I wrote Percy's fire report and got him an extra twenty thousand. I agreed to do the report and he agreed to pay five thousand. And all he had was fire damage in his bedroom. If I hadn't doctored up the report, the insurance company would've only given him five thousand dollars, if that. That's just how the insurance companies operate. They make you pay them millions of dollars in policy fees, but they only want to pay you pennies when fires and robberies happen. They are bigger crooks than anyone I know. That's why the scam me and Tim have is foolproof. We get the homeowner paid and they, in turn, pay us. Is that a sweat deal or what?

Now don't get me wrong, we have had some people who tried to buck on us and threaten not to pay. But as soon as we dangle the words "insurance fraud," and the time that they could get if we blew the whistle on them, they shape up and wanna do right by us. Money is a terrible drug. And I happen to be one of the ones that enjoy having it come through my hands.

My next stop was the old man that lived in Lake Edward. I could tell when we first approached him with the scheme, he was gamed at the door. He looked like he was hurting for money, and Tim and I both saw it too. Mr. Cole was a cross between a slickster and a gambler. So Tim and I knew what we were dealing with when we got him to agree to let us help him. He was all smiles when we told him about our services. He acted like he had just made two new best friends. He even called Tim and me his newfound sons.

When I pulled up to the old man's house, surprisingly, he was sitting outside on his front porch. After I parked my car behind his car in the driveway, I climbed out of it and closed the door. Once I emerged from my car, he recognized me.

"Mr. Riddick," he said.

"How are you, Mr. Cole?" I asked as I walked up the walkway to his house.

"I'm doing good. What brings you by?" he wanted to know.

"I came by to collect," I told him as I made my way onto his porch.

"Collect what?"

"The money you owe me."

"I don't owe you anything," he replied sarcastically.

"No, you do owe me money, Mr. Cole. And you agreed to pay me twenty-five thousand dollars for the report I sent to your insurance company."

"That was until I found out that you were trying to rip me off."

"What do you mean 'rip off'?"

"I talked to my daughter about it and she said that I didn't have to pay you anything."

"Where is your daughter now?"

"She's not here. She's at work."

"Mr. Cole, I need my money."

"Well, son, I hate to be the bearer of bad news, but I ain't giving you shit. See, that's what's wrong with you young people. Always trying to get over on senior citizens. But not tonight. I'm not giving you a dime."

Alonzo laughed. "You're joking, right?"

"Do I look like I'm joking?"

"Mr. Cole, I'm not leaving here without my money."

"Oh, yes, the fuck you are, and you're gonna get off my property right now or else I'll call the cops and have you removed!" he roared, and stood up on his feet.

"You do know that as soon as you call the cops, I'm gonna tell them about our arrangement? I'm gonna tell them about your involvement."

"I don't give a fuck. Tell 'em. And who you think they're gonna believe? Me or you?"

"They're gonna believe me."

"So you're telling me that you're gonna implicate your own self just to get me arrested?"

"If that's what it takes," I told him.

"I don't believe you."

"Then call them and test me," I dared him.

"Get off my property right now," he instructed me. And his volume got louder and I didn't want him bringing attention to our dispute. All I wanted to do was collect the money and leave. It was as simple as that.

"I'm sorry, but I can't do that, Mr. Cole. I need my money."

I looked at Mr. Cole from head to toe, sizing him up. He was about five-eight in height. His weight couldn't be more than 165 pounds, if that. And he used a cane to help him get around. If I decided to snuff this motherfucker out, it wouldn't take much. "So you're saying that you're not paying me?" I wanted him to clarify his intent.

"You must be out of your fucking mind if you think that I am going to give you twenty-five thousand dollars. The insurance company only gave me fifty to fix my kitchen and back den. So, do you think that I'm gonna give you half of that?"

"When I wrote your report, I exaggerated the damages. That's why you got more than what you were supposed to get. So a deal is a deal."

"Young man, if you don't get off my porch, I am going to call the cops on your Black ass right now." He threatened me once again and then proceeded toward me. He met me at the edge of the porch and we stood before one another, face-to-face.

"So you aren't gonna pay me anything?"

"I'm not giving you shit. Now get!" he shouted.

I turned around slowly to survey the area around Mr. Cole's front porch. When it appeared to me that no one was around, I turned back and faced Mr. Cole, and then I jabbed him in his throat with my fist. *Boom!* Mr. Cole grabbed his neck with his left hand, his eyes went to the back of his head, and then he fell down on the front porch. I looked down at him and it appeared that he had stopped breathing. I bent down to check his pulse, but the old man wasn't breathing, and I instantly panicked. "Fuck! Did I just kill this old man?" I said aloud. I stood there in shock and then I questioned myself, not knowing what to do. One part of me wanted to run back to my car and leave, but then I had to remind myself that I had come all the way over here to collect the money that was owed to me and Tim, so I had to get it by any means necessary. But then I also thought about the chances of how I was going to get it when the old man was dead. Then it dawned on me that he might have something lingering around the house. I remembered back to when I came by after the fire and wrote up the report, he was upset that the fire happened, because he had a poker game that same night. So, I figured, he's gotta have a stash somewhere.

Thinking quickly on my feet, I ran back to my car, grabbed my work gloves from my glove compartment, slipped them on, and raced back onto the porch. I opened the front screen door, grabbed Mr. Cole by his arms, and dragged him into his house. After I got him in and away from the front door, I closed and locked it. Panting heavily, I went straight to his bedroom and looked everywhere I thought that he would keep his money. And what do you know? As soon as I looked in his closet, I found a fireproof lockbox. I picked it up and realized that it was heavy. And when I tried to open it, I saw that I needed a key, so with the lockbox in hand, I raced back to the front of the house, where Mr. Cole was lying on the floor. I noticed that he had a set of keys hanging from a lanyard attached to his belt, so I unclipped it and sifted through the keys to see which one would fit the lockbox. After trying the fourth key, I struck gold and was able to open the box. When I opened it, I was surprised to see the amount of money inside. There had to be at least fifteen thousand. I took all seven stacks of tens, twenties, fifties, and hundreds, and stuffed them all into the waste area of my pants. And then I raced back to the old man's bedroom closet and placed the box inside, like how I had found it. I didn't want to bring any attention to the lockbox by leaving it where the old man was. If I had, the daughter would know right off the bat that it was a robbery and would call the cops as soon as she saw her father lying on the floor dead.

With the money safely secured in my pocket, I made my exit. Thankfully, when I walked out of the home, no one was around, at least to my knowledge. So I got in my car and headed back to the station.

As soon as I pulled into the parking lot of the station and parked my car, I pulled out the money and began to count it. At the end of the count, I realized that I had nineteen thousand dollars in my possession. It wasn't the twenty-five thousand dollars that the old man owed us, but it was more than two-thirds of it. That's better than nothing. After I finished the count, I divided the money into ninety-five hundred dollars each, placed my portion in my glove compartment, and stuffed Tim's part back into my waist area of my pants. When I exited my car, it dawned on me that I had a dead man's money in my pocket. I really just killed an old man. But then I had to remind myself that he owed me money, and under no circumstances was he going to give it to me. So, what was I going to do? Just let him get away with it? That's not what we agreed on. He owed us, so he had to pay up. Sorry that he lost his life in the process, but that's just how things work. You don't pay, you don't live. It's as simple as that. But the thing that loomed over my head was, should I tell Tim or not? How would he react if he found out I had to kill the old man to get our money? Another question, would he rat me out? I couldn't have another man holding cards in his hands that could throw me in prison for life. So I decided it would be best to keep this secret close to my vest. And when the news made the report about his death, I'd just deny it. I'd say that it must've happened after I picked up the money. He'd believe me because I'd never done anything like that before.

"Tim, I've got a gift for you," I said after I appeared in the entryway of his office.

He beamed like a child on Christmas Day. "Well, come on in," he insisted. "And close my door."

After I closed his office door, I pulled out his money and placed it on top of his desk. "How much is this?"

"Nine thousand five hundred dollars."

"This is from the old man?" he asked me.

"Yep," I replied, and took a seat in one of the chairs in front of his desk.

"What did he say when you went to his house?"

"Nothing, really. He said that he'd been waiting on me to stop by," I lied.

"Did he say when he was going to pay us the rest?"

I sighed. "See, that's the thing. Nineteen grand was all he had left. So I took it and left." I lied once more. I had to paint the narrative that the old man ran out of money, so there would be no need to go back over there to collect anything else. And besides, he was dead. How would I look going back? That would definitely create some suspicion for the daughter, and I couldn't have that.

"That fucking piece of shit! Does he know that we lied on his report so that he could get more money from his insurance company?" Tim questioned me.

"I told him that. And he told me that he runs a gambling spot at his home and he lost a lot of his money. What he gave me was all he had left." My lies continued.

"I'm glad you went over there. Because if I had gone over there and he told me that bullshit, I might've choked his ass out." He spoke through gritted teeth.

I chuckled mischievously, because I was guilty as charged. "Look on the bright side, we got something. Who knows? He may not have had anything if I'd waited longer to go over there."

"Thank God for that." Tim finally agreed and then he put his money in the bottom drawer of his desk.

"Anything happen since I was gone?" I changed the subject.

"No. We all ate dinner. But that's about it."

"Talk to Kirsten since she left?"

"Yeah, she called me once."

"Was she fussing?"

"It started off that way, but I calmed her down."

"Can I ask you a question?"

"Sure."

"Are you and my sister having an affair?"

Tim burst into laughter. "Did you ask me and your sister this same question before you left the station?"

"Yeah, I did. But we're alone now. And I'm coming to you, man to man."

"Well, the answer is the same as before. I am not sleeping with Alayna. I told you, she's like a little sister to me."

"You're giving me your word?"

"Yes, Alonzo, I'm giving you my word," Tim assured me.

I sat there and searched his face for a second. He seemed sincere with his answer, so I chalked it up to what it was, nothing. "Have you processed the other two reports from last week's fires?" I wanted to know.

"Yep, I've got copies of them right here." He slid two documents he retrieved from a folder on his desk.

I picked up both reports and scanned them from top to bottom. "Looks like Mr. Pearson is gonna get a full payout," I noted.

"Yeah, his whole house was torched. But guess what?"

"What?"

"He committed arson, and while I was inspecting the damages, he was there and I confronted him about it. He tried to deny it, but I told him his secret is safe with me, but he was going to have to pay up. He agreed to pay us one hundred grand."

"What was his house worth?"

"The value of his home was around half a million."

"Oh, he's got a huge payday coming."

"Exactly. And so do we," Tim corrected me.

I chuckled. "I love the sound of *ka-ching*," I commented, and then I placed the first report behind the second one and started reading the contents of it. "I remember this young couple's house. Their fire started in the kitchen. It was a grease fire."

"Yeah, but I made it look like she had extensive damages to the entire kitchen," Tim pointed out.

"I see. And judging from this, they might get seventy-five grand."

"They could get more."

"You're right, they could." I agreed. "Want me to run these reports over to them now?" I added.

"Nah, it's too late. Wait until tomorrow."

"Roger that," I said, and placed both reports back on Tim's desk.

Feeling hunger pains in my stomach, I stood up from my chair. "I guess I'm gonna head in the kitchen and get me some of that spaghetti."

"You better. It's good."

"Say no more," I said, and then I exited his office. As I walked towards the kitchen, I wondered to myself if Tim will realize that I didn't give him a portion of the money I collected from Percy? I'll tell you what, won't mention it, unless he does.

CHAPTER 6

Alayna

"**H**EY, YOU," MY BROTHER SAID AS HE ENTERED THE KITCHEN. I was wiping down the tables when he walked in.

"Where's the food?" he wanted to know, rubbing both of his hands together.

"In the refrigerator."

He opened the refrigerator, grabbed the container of leftover spaghetti, and placed it into the microwave. While it was heating up, he sat down in one of the seats at the table and started up a conversation about why I was so down all of a sudden. I tried to dismiss it, as if I was tired, but he wasn't buying that. He was my brother. He knew me. He knew when something was wrong with me. "You and Tim were having an affair, weren't you?"

"No, we weren't." I tried to stay busy with the cleaning towel. I tried avoiding eye contact with him too. But he got up from the table and approached me. He even took the cleaning towel out of my hand and made me face him.

"Alayna, tell me the truth. I won't get mad. Just tell me what's going on."

I dropped my head low. But he grabbed my chin and lifted it back up. "You slept with him, didn't you?" he repeated. He wasn't letting up.

I nodded my head.

He stood there in complete shock. He even gave me a look of disappointment. "Why, Alayna?"

I shrugged my shoulders, but that wasn't enough for him. He wanted answers.

"Talk to me, sis. Tell me what made you do that? He has a fucking wife and you have a husband. And, besides, you're in your fucking twenties. He's almost old enough to be your fucking father."

"I don't know. I mean, it just happened," I finally said. That was the only answer I could come up with.

"You know he took cold advantage of you? And that's fucked up. I thought we were family," Alonzo commented. He was getting angrier by the second. "I'm gonna go and talk to that motherfucker right now. He knows better," he insisted, and then he abruptly broke away from me and turned to leave. But I grabbed ahold of his hand.

"Please don't. There's been enough drama today. Just let it go. He said that we can't be together anymore, so there you go. It's over and it will never happen again," I explained.

"So he broke up with you, huh?" Alonzo said sarcastically.

"Look, it's not about who broke up with who. The main issue here is that we're not gonna see each other anymore. It's over."

"It better be, because if I found out otherwise, I'm saying something, and it ain't gonna be nice," Alonzo warned me. "Wait, you know what . . ." he said, and then paused. "I'm gonna address this now." He snatched away from me once more. He belled out of the kitchen and raced to Tim's office. I ran behind him, but I couldn't get to him in time before he burst into Tim's office. From the direction I was coming from, I could see into Tim's office after Alonzo made his way inside, but I couldn't see Tim. I heard a lot of commotion though. "What the fuck are you doing, coming in here like that? Are you out of your mind?" I heard Tim say.

"What kind of shit you got going on in here?" Alonzo asked.

By this time, I was only a couple feet away. Alonzo heard my steps and looked back over his shoulders. "Sis, come look at this shit."

"Alonzo, get out of my office right now before I have your job!"

Tim threatened Alonzo, but my brother wouldn't move. He grabbed me by the arm and pulled me into the entryway of Tim's office, and my eyes immediately landed on Tim buttoning up his pants. With a guilty look on his face, Jesse stood beside Tim, not able to make eye contact with any of us.

"I just caught ole Jesse giving Tim some top."

"Some what?" I asked Tim. I needed clarity.

Tim started walking toward his office door. "Leave my office right now," he instructed us.

"Some head. Tim had homeboy giving him some head," Alonzo clarified for me, talking over Tim's voice. I immediately became sick to my stomach. Before Tim reached the doorway, I turned around and ran back down the hallway. Instead of going back into the kitchen, I raced to my room to get away from everyone. En route, I heard Alonzo and Tim start a verbal altercation in the distance.

"You nasty son of a bitch! And here I was coming to chew you out about taking advantage of my sister and fucking her. But you ain't loyal to nobody. Got ole Jesse here giving you some head during work hours. I wonder what everyone is going to say once I tell them this."

"Get away from my office door now!" I heard Tim roar, and then the sirens went off and I couldn't hear Tim or Alonzo's mouth over the fire alarm. My first thought was to go and suit up to leave with the guys, but I knew I couldn't face Tim. Not right now. So I continued on into my room and let the big boys handle the fire they were getting ready to leave for.

After the guys left the station, I turned on the TV and lay in my bed and thought about what Tim was doing with Jesse. The visual in my head was unbearable and I realized that it was best that I didn't see those guys in action. To actually see it would've traumatized me. What's even more devastating was that Tim was having sex with me and with Jesse. How fucked up is that? This guy was bisexual. Oh, my God! What was I going to do now? Was I going to be able to get past this? Was I going to be able to work with Tim and Jesse, knowing what I knew now? I felt so fucking heartbroken and I knew that I was gonna need some days off behind this. Yeah, that's exactly what I needed.

While I was lying in bed, my husband, Levi, called me. I didn't want to take his call, but I figured that by talking to him, he could probably get my mind off what was going on around here.

"Hello," I answered.

"Hey, whatcha doing?" he started the conversation off.

"Nothing much. Just lying here in my bed."

"Where is everybody else?"

"They just got a call, so I'm here alone."

"What's wrong? You don't sound like yourself."

"I'm just tired. I cleaned up the truck port, rearranged supplies, and cleaned up the kitchen after everyone ate."

"Got a call from my mother. She wants us to come by and spend Mother's Day with her. What do you think?"

"Do you plan on taking her out?"

"Yeah, that crossed my mind. And I also want to get that painting she likes from that art gallery in Norfolk."

"Levi, that thing costs a thousand dollars."

"We have it."

"No, I have it. That's my money in the bank."

"So that's what we're doing?"

"Levi, just get her something else. Like a pair of Ugg boots. Or a cute little gold bracelet."

"We got her a gold bracelet for Christmas," Levi replied sarcastically. He was not feeling me or what I was saying. Anytime I went against his mother, he had a hard time dealing with it. But see, he didn't make a lot of money as a school PE coach. So I took the reins and took over our finances with the money that my dad left me. Levi didn't like it, but he had no choice in the matter.

"Look, Levi, can we talk about this later?"

"No, we're gonna talk about it now."

"Well, then it's final. She's not getting the painting. Get her something else. Something that you can afford."

"You know what? You never let shit go my way. I betcha if I were Tim, you wouldn't give me such a hard time."

"But you're not Tim."

"So it's true? You are fucking him?"

"No, I'm not fucking him. He's fucking another firefighter, Jesse," I slipped up and said. And when I realized that I had spilled the tea, Levi burst into laughter.

"Tim is gay?" Levi questioned me.

"I don't know what Tim is."

"How do you know he's poking the other dude?" Levi continued to chuckle.

"Alonzo caught them in the act."

"What were they doing?"

"Alonzo said that Jesse was giving Tim some head in his office while the door was closed."

"No way. And here I thought Tim was banging you. I swear, I didn't see that."

I wanted to comment, but I didn't. Regardless of what Levi knew, I was actually allowing Tim to bang me, so the freaking joke was on him. I, on the other hand, felt sick in my stomach, knowing that Tim was having sex with me and Jesse too. The thing I didn't know was how long it was going on.

"Wow! I'm blown away. I wonder if his wife knows whether he prefers dick or pussy?" he added.

"Look, I don't wanna talk about this anymore," I told Levi. Because at this point, the topic wasn't funny.

"Is this your way of getting off the phone?" he wanted to know.

"Levi, I told you that I was tired. Please let me get some rest. I'll talk to you later," I replied, and then I ended the call. He tried to call my cell phone back, but I refused to answer it. He then sent two text messages, but I refused to read them. I figured that he was going on one of his rants and I wasn't going to be a part of it. I had too much on my mind right now to entertain his bullshit. Especially with him wanting to spend one thousand dollars to purchase his mother a freaking painting from the money that Tim had given me. Levi must be out of his mind. And his mother too if she thought that she was gonna manipulate him into buying it. Not on my watch.

The guys returned to the station about an hour and a half later. Alonzo came looking for me immediately after he got undressed. "Was there a fire?" I asked him after he entered my room.

"No, there was an elderly woman that passed out from a gas leak in her home. But we got her back breathing. The paramedics put her on an oxygen machine and took her to Sentara Hospital for further treatment." Alonzo sat down on the edge of the twin-size bed I was lying on.

"Where is Tim?" I asked.

"He's in his office."

"Did you really catch Jesse giving him head?"

"Yeah, sis, I did. And I still can't fucking believe it."

"Has he said anything to you about it since y'all left?"

"No, we haven't talked at all."

"What about Jesse? Has he said anything to you?"

"Nope. He's been avoiding me. While Tim, myself, and Paul was in the old lady's house, Jesse stayed outside."

"That's because he's embarrassed."

"I would be too if another dude caught me sucking off another dude's dick."

"Ahhhhhh, don't say it like that. That sounds nasty."

"How else do you want me to say it?"

"Just don't say it at all. As a matter of fact, I don't even wanna talk about it anymore. The whole thing is disgusting."

"I'm gonna tell his wife."

"Who? Kirsten?"

"Yeah, the next time she comes up here, I'm gonna tell her that her man is getting sucked off by Jesse, not you."

"No, Zo, you can't say that. Tim will fire you for that," I warned him.

"Tim can't fire me. Only the mayor can fire me, so I can say what I wanna say."

"But Tim can still vote you out of here."

"I wish he would. With all the shit I got on him, he wouldn't dare."

"What do you have on him?"

"If only you knew," Alonzo said, and then his focus turned toward the twenty-seven-inch flat-screen TV on the dresser in the room I was in. It was breaking news. Alonzo got up from my bed and turned up the volume, using the remote control I had placed on the lamp stand next to my bed.

"*In breaking news this evening, the Virginia Beach Police Department is here at a residence on Lake Edward Drive, in the Lake Edward neighborhood, where a daughter came home from work and found her father dead on the floor by the front door. From what I'm told, there's not cause of death, but homicide detectives are on-site and will do a thorough investigation. No name has been released for the deceased, because other family members need to be notified. The daughter has asked for privacy so that she can deal with this matter. This is Karen Taylor, coming to you live from WTKR.*"

"The old guy probably had a heart attack," I said.

"Yeah, looks that way."

"But, wait, didn't we put out a fire at that house?" I asked.

"Yeah, it looks familiar." Alonzo somewhat agreed with my observation.

"I thought so," I added.

Alonzo stood up from my bed. "I guess I'll get up and go to the bathroom. Been holding this thing since we left."

"Please take care of that. Don't wanna see you having an accident on my floor."

Alonzo chuckled. "And neither do I," he said, and then he kissed me on the forehead and left.

CHAPTER 7

Tim

I HAD JESSE COME IN MY OFFICE AFTER WE CAME BACK FROM OUR field call. After he walked into my office, I closed the door and locked it behind him. "Have a seat," I instructed him. He sat down on the small sofa I had in the corner of my office. I sat down next to him. "You know we need to talk about what happened earlier."

"Yes, I know. But what is there to say?"

"You haven't been working here that long, so I want to prepare you if Alonzo starts to harass you about what he saw earlier. Because he can be an asshole. I know, I've been working with him for over fifteen years."

"I understand you want to help, but I can handle myself."

"But you don't know Alonzo. He can get underneath your skin and make you want to deck him in the face."

"I don't think that he could get me that upset that I'd want to hit him." Jesse refuted what I was saying, but he didn't know Alonzo like I did. Alonzo has a way to say things that would make a person want to kill him. His mouth has always been foul, and the quicker Jesse realized this, the better he'd be prepared and know how to handle Alonzo—if they ever had words with one another.

"Okay. I've officially warned you. So don't come complaining to me if things go south with you two."

"Don't worry, I won't," Jesse assured me, and then stood up. "If you need me, I'll be in my room."

"Think you could stop by my room later?"

"Why don't you get Alayna to stop by your room," he responded sarcastically.

"Are you serious right now?"

Jesse stopped in front of my office door. "You lied to me. You told me that you and Alayna weren't seeing each other. But you were. So I'm done with you."

"Well, be done then. And close my door after you leave."

Without saying another word, I watched Jesse leave my office. And there I was, all out of playthings. No Alayna and no Jesse. But it was okay. I'd find someone else to play with, because I always get what I want. What one person won't do, the next person will, and I wouldn't have it no other way.

CHAPTER 8

Alonzo

SINCE I HADN'T EATEN ALL DAY, I MADE MY WAY BACK IN THE kitchen, where I left the leftover spaghetti in the microwave. After I powered on the microwave to warm up the food, Paul entered the kitchen. "Smells good in here," he said. Paul was a cool guy. He was a young half-Asian/half-white guy who volunteered for us, and he was doing really good here. Almost lost him one time in a huge fire we had to battle, a few months back, but we all banded together and brought him to safety. There was no way we could tell his mother that her twenty-five-year-old son had died in a fire we were fighting. That's not the news we like to deliver to our firefighters' families.

"I'm warming up some leftovers. Care to have some?" I asked him after grabbing a paper plate from the pantry.

"Nah, I'm good. I'm gonna get a bottle of water," he told me while grabbing one from the refrigerator. After opening the bottle, he took a seat at the table. "What was all the commotion about earlier?" he wanted to know.

I chuckled. "I wish I could tell you. I swear, it would blow your mind."

"I'm sure you will," Paul replied, and smiled.

"Talking about me?" I heard a voice say from across the room. Paul and I looked in that direction, and what do you know?

Jesse was standing there like he was upset with the world. "Nah, we weren't talking about you. But we could start a conversation about you if you like," I assured him while I grabbed my food from the microwave and a fork from the utensil drawer.

"I'm sure you could," Jesse stated; then he exited the kitchen.

Paul looked at me again and burst into laughter. By this time, I was dumping a pile of spaghetti onto my plate. "What was that all about?" Paul wondered aloud.

"If I'm not mistaken, I'd think that he was trying to intimidate me," I responded; then I set the bowl down on the table next to my plate. "But if he knew like I knew, he'd be better off leaving me alone, because I'll blow up his whole spot," I added, and then I dug my fork into my food and started eating it.

Paul laughed. "Y'all be good now. Don't want to place white sheets over any bodies around here."

"If there's a body to lay a sheet over, it won't be mine. I can guarantee you on that one," I told Paul, and then I shoved a mouthful of spaghetti in my mouth.

Paul and I talked a little more and then he excused himself and retreated to his room. I stayed back in the kitchen and scarfed down another plate of spaghetti, until I got full and couldn't eat another bite. Afterward, I headed into the TV room to monitor the news. Nothing else popped up about the old man, so I kept my fingers crossed that the detectives on that case would rule his death from natural causes—and not murder.

I had been in the TV room for at least thirty minutes alone and then Tim arrived. The energy was awkward, especially since it was only he and I in the room. I tried to pretend like I was engrossed in the television show I was watching, but that didn't matter to Tim. He wanted to clear the air, so he broke the ice.

"Can I talk to you outside the station?" he asked.

I turned my head in his direction. "Why can't we talk here? I'm watching TV."

"Because I need this to be a private conversation."

"Ain't nobody in here but me and you, so talk."

"I prefer we talk outside. So do me that favor, please."

I hesitated for a moment, because I wanted to tell that dude to kiss my ass and go outside by himself. But for the sake of privacy, I got up from the sofa and went outside with him.

As soon as we exited the building, we walked over to the picnic table. I sat down on the table with my feet on the bench, and Tim stood a few feet away from me, with his arms folded and pressed against his chest.

"So, what do you want to talk about?" I asked. But I already knew what it was about. The dude was embarrassed about me catching another dude sucking on his meat and now he wanted to justify his actions. Maybe even tell me that what I saw was not what really happened. Tim had a way of making you question yourself, but he wouldn't do that shit to me. Not now, not ever.

"I wanna talk about what happened in my office."

"I'm listening."

"Well, I know what you saw and I can't change that. But out of respect for me, Jesse, and your sister, I'm asking you to keep it to yourself. No one else in this station needs to know what happened."

I laughed out loud. "So you're ashamed?"

"No, I'm not ashamed. I just think that what happened earlier is no one else's business."

I nodded my head, because he was right. What happened earlier was his business. But my sister is my business—and he had some explaining to do about that. "You know what, you're right. Me catching Jesse sucking you off is your business. But why did you lie to me? I asked you if you were sleeping with my sister and you looked in my face and lied to me. I thought that we were better than that. I thought that we were brothers, Tim. But you're showing me a different side to you."

"Listen, brother—"

I cut him off in midsentence. "Tim, I'm not your brother. You fucked that up when you lied to me."

"Zo, it was Alayna's idea not to say anything to anyone. I told her a long time ago that we should tell you what was going on between us."

"I don't wanna hear that shit, Tim. You took advantage of my sister. You're damn near old enough to be her father, dude. Come on . . . stop playing victim."

"I'm not trying to play the victim. I was only honoring her wishes."

"No, you were trying to cover your ass. Meanwhile, you got your wife acting like a damn fool, trying to attack my sister. Does she know that you like dudes too?" My tone got a little stronger. I needed him to hear the anger in my voice, because I was appalled by his actions.

"No, she doesn't."

"I wonder what she would say if she found out that you're fucking with a dude that you brought on as a recently hired firefighter?"

"So you're threatening me right now that you're going to tell her?"

"Nah, bro, I ain't threatening you. That's you and her business. But what I will say is, if I found out that you're fucking with my sister again, then we're going to have some serious problems."

"Yeah, I can take that. But before you go off and do something crazy, remember that you and I have a side business together and I will take you down with me."

I slid off the picnic table and gave Tim one hard look in the face without saying a word. After five seconds of giving him a hard stare, I walked away from him and headed back into the station.

"You better not harass Jesse either. Leave him out of this!" Tim shouted from behind as the door to the station closed. All I could do was shake my head. He was a slick dude and now I was starting to see who he really was. For him to threaten to bring me down with him gave me confirmation that I did the right thing by not telling him that I murdered the old man. If he knew, he'd probably be on the phone right now, calling the cops and ratting me out. But whether he knew it or not, I'd kill him first before I rotted in a jail. So he better be careful.

I'd normally tell Tim when I make a field run, but after what had transpired earlier, I knew to stay as far away from him, for as long as I could. He knew that I was going to pick up the money from Ms. Whitney, so I left the station and headed in her direction.

I wanted to make it over there by midnight. Didn't want her to think I was intrusive if I went by her place after that. Thankfully, she was up walking around her house when I rang the doorbell. She let me in the house. Ms. Whitney was a white woman in her midthirties. She was a piece of eye candy, but I dared not cross that line, especially when we were doing this business deal.

"Come on in," she insisted, and I walked into her home.

She lived in a two-level town house and I wrote her paperwork as a fifty-thousand-dollar claim, even though she only had about ten thousand dollars' worth of damages. My cut was fifteen thousand. She had already given half of it to me a week ago.

"I have your cash right here," she said, handing me a manila envelope. I stood near the front door as she handed me the money.

I grabbed it and placed it in my back pocket. "Thank you," I said.

"You're welcome. Come on into the kitchen and let me show you what I did with some of the money," she insisted, so I followed her. She showed me a new gas stove and a stainless-steel microwave and refrigerator too.

"You gotta go big or go home," she commented.

"Nice. See you had the walls painted a whole different color."

"Yeah, I did. And that's only because I couldn't find the original paint color. I'm kind of glad that I did, because I otherwise wouldn't have changed it to this color."

"Yes, this is better." I admired it.

"Want something to drink? Coke. Juice. You name it, I got it. Thanks to you."

I chuckled. "No, don't give me that much credit."

"Well, if you hadn't done what you did, then I wouldn't have that extra money in my pocket to tie up a lot of loose ends around my place. This was really a blessing to me."

"Don't mention it."

"I know a couple of people that'll do the same thing I did, if you need the referral."

"Are they trustworthy?"

"Of course, they are. They're family. My own flesh and blood."

"Well, then set it up."

"Would they need to set the fire on their own?"

"Let me talk to them first. I don't want them doing something that they'll regret later. Doing that sort of thing could get tricky. You gotta know what you're doing."

"Okay, then I'll set it up."

"You do that. And I'm gonna get out of your hair. Gotta get back to the station."

"You take care."

"You do the same," I told the woman, and then I bounced.

CHAPTER 9

Alayna

KNOCK! KNOCK! KNOCK! WHEN I HEARD THE KNOCKING ON my door, my first thought was, either it was my brother coming back in here to check on me, or it was Tim.

"Who is it?" I asked, after realizing that I had dozed off while watching TV.

"It's Tim. Can I come in?"

See, I fucking knew it. I knew it had to be him or my brother. But the way I was feeling, I didn't want to be bothered. I wanted to be alone and not deal with any of his bullshit. I also knew that if I told him to go away, he was not gonna listen. He was going to stand there at my door until I let him in and let him say what it was he wanted to say. So I went against my better judgment and allowed him to enter my room.

"Yes, you can come in," I finally said.

The door opened and he stepped inside. He closed the door and stood there in the middle of the floor. I sat up on my bed, with my legs crossed, and waited for him to say whatever it was that he came here to say.

"Are you all right?" he started off saying.

"I'm fine. Now tell me why you're here?" I got straight to the point. I wasn't in the mood to let him drag this on.

"I came in here to apologize to you."

"What exactly are you apologizing for?"

"For what happened earlier when your brother saw me and Jesse in that compromising position. I know that must've hurt you."

"I know you personally brought him on as a firefighter, but how long have you two been seeing each other in that way?"

"For a while now."

"What's 'for a while now,' Tim? Six months? One year? Two years?" I spat. My pitch got a little higher. He was annoying the hell out of me.

"Two and a half years now, I think."

"Are you fucking kidding me? So you've been fucking with that guy for that long? Does Kirsten know that?"

"Of course, she doesn't."

"So, if you've been fucking with him that long, then why did you start messing around with me? Wasn't him and your wife enough?"

"It was just something about you that I had to have." He tried to explain, but I wasn't trying to hear that bullshit!

"So you think it's okay to sleep with a man and a woman? Well, let me correct that—one man and two women."

"I can't help that I love what I love."

"And that's your excuse, Tim. Do you know how nasty that is? It was bad enough that you were sleeping with two women, but to add a man to the mix is just disgusting. And it's dangerous. Now I've gotta go and take an HIV test and pray to God that I don't have the virus. Levi would fucking kill me!" I told him as tears welled up in my eyes. And then, one by one, they started falling down my face.

"Please don't cry. I am so sorry."

"You know what, Tim? Keep your 'I'm sorry' and get out of my room. Just the sight of you is making me sick to my stomach."

"So that's it? That's how you want to leave things?"

"There's nothing else to say. As a matter of fact, I'm going to use some of my leave and take off the next three or four days. I need some time alone to pull myself back together."

"Okay. That's fine. I'll give you that," he said willingly, and then exited my room.

Like a teenage girl that just broke up with her high school sweetheart, I buried my face in my pillow and started crying my eyes out. My heart was so broken and I felt like shit. And all I could think about was, how stupid could I have been? I let this older man woo me, and then, boom, break my heart, not one but two times. And here Kirsten thought he was just having an affair with me. I wonder how she'd feel if she knew he was having an affair with his mentee, Jesse? I knew that would blow her mind. Boy, would I pay to see her face. But then I figured, why pay when I could see it for free? Now it was only a matter of time.

CHAPTER 10

Tim

AFTER MY FAILED APOLOGY TO ALAYNA, I HEADED TO MY ROOM and tried to get some rest before we got another emergency call. Once inside my room, I powered on the TV and watched a couple of legal-program reruns, and when they ended, I found the TV watching me instead of me watching it. But then I was drawn back to the television when a special news report interrupted the regular broadcasting show. I sat up on my bed and tuned in.

> *"In breaking news, we are outside the home of Mr. David Cole, a retired truck driver, who was found dead by his daughter after she came there from work. After further investigation, this case has been ruled as a homicide and robbery. The daughter of the deceased indicated that her father kept money in his fireproof safe, but when she looked in it, it was empty. I had the daughter on camera earlier and this is what she had to say."*
>
> *"When I came home and saw my father dead on the floor, I initially thought that he had had a heart attack or something. But when the detective called me and told me that my father had a lot of bruising in the center of his throat, they examined it and that's when they realized that he was hit there and it damaged his windpipe and cut off his oxygen. It*

immediately became apparent that he was attacked. Now, I can't say why someone would do this to my father, because he was a good man. He would give you the shirt off his back. We just had a house fire a couple months back and I almost lost him in that. I don't know where all of this bad luck is coming from, but I need it to stop. So, if anybody knows or seen anything, please call Detectives Mark Granger and Evan Richards. I need justice for my father, so, again, if you seen anyone come here or a car that you remember seeing, please call them. And thank you so much." The daughter stopped speaking and the interview ended.

"Well, you heard it here first. The deceased's daughter, Sabrina Cole, asking for help to find the suspect that murdered her father. She also indicated that money was stolen from a fireproof safe he owned. I asked a couple of neighbors, off camera, if they saw anything, and only one of them said that they saw Mr. Cole sitting on his porch alone, but they never saw him go inside his home. They also said that they saw a car in Mr. Cole's driveway sometime later and then it was gone. No one else could give me any information. So, if you know or saw anything, please call the hotline, 1-800-LOCK-U-UP. I am Karen Taylor, coming to you live from WTKR."

I sat there in shock as I listened to the broadcast. I knew instantly that Alonzo definitely had to have had something to do with Mr. Cole's death. But why? Why would he kill the man? Was he not willing to give up the money he owed us? I needed to talk to Alonzo and find out what really happened when he went there, because I'd be damned if I took the fall with him if the cops found out that he had something to do with that man's murder.

I took a deep breath, exhaled, and then I stood up, slipped on my shoes, and went to look for Alonzo. I went to his room and knocked on the door, but he wasn't there, so I went to the kitchen and he wasn't in there either. When I entered the lounge area, Alonzo was sitting on the sofa, alone, watching TV. I sat down on the opposite end of the sofa and told him that we needed to talk.

"What do we need to talk about now?" he asked me.

"I just saw the news. The old man you picked up the money from is dead."

"Yeah, I saw that. That's tragic."

"They said that he was murdered. And his daughter was interviewed by a news reporter, and she told her that her father was robbed. So they're calling this a robbery and homicide."

"Am I supposed to care?"

"Did you kill that old man?"

"No, I didn't."

"Did you rob him?"

"No."

"So, what happened?"

"What do you mean?"

"What did you say to the man? How did he give you the money, and where was he at when you left?"

"Why do I have to explain all of that to you? I didn't kill the man, and that's it."

"One of the neighbors said that they saw a car parked in the driveway. So you better hope they don't identify your car as *that car*," I warned him.

"Look, I don't care what the neighbor saw. When I went there, the old man was sitting on the porch. I greeted him and reminded him why I was there. He told me that he was waiting for me to come by and get the money, so he got up from the chair, went in the house, and returned a few minutes later with the money. I took it, thanked him, and then I left. It was that cut-and-dry," Alonzo finally explained.

"So you're saying that the old man didn't resist, and you didn't have to take the money from him?"

"No. He said that he had the money tucked away in a little lockbox safe, so he could pay me, and even though he didn't have all of what he owed us, he gave me everything he had left."

I started believing him until he said the words "lockbox safe." How in the world did he know that the money was in a safe? Unless he took the money from that safe himself. My gut told me that Alonzo wasn't telling me everything. And the more I looked at him sitting there on that sofa, the more I was inclined to believe that he robbed the man, and the man threatened to call the cops, so Alonzo hit him in his throat, damaging his windpipe and killing him on the spot.

I stood up from the sofa, because I knew that Alonzo wasn't going to say anything more about the situation. But I did leave him with this: "For your sake, I hope you didn't rob or kill that old man."

"And what is that supposed to mean?" He became defensive.

"I'm just saying that you could get life in prison for robbery and murder."

"So I heard," he replied sarcastically.

I heard him mumble something else underneath his breath, but it was not audible enough for me to hear it clearly. My first thought was to ask him to repeat himself. But then I figured that it would start up another verbal altercation with him and I wasn't in the mood. I had had enough of his mouth for one day. So I made my exit and headed back to my room.

CHAPTER 11

Alonzo

IMMEDIATELY AFTER TIM LEFT THE TV ROOM, I STARTED FEELING knots in my stomach. The fact that the cops knew that Mr. Cole's death wasn't a heart attack, and that it was a robbery and murder, got me worried. And for the neighbor to see a car in the driveway spooked me too. What if they identified my car as the one that was there during the time that old man was killed? Man, what was I going to do now?

While pondering how I was going to move forward concerning this situation, my cell phone started ringing. I looked at the caller ID and saw that my fiancée, Pricilla, was calling. "What's up, baby?"

"I saw a couple of white guys sitting in a car outside our terrace apartment about ten minutes ago, and when I just looked back outside, I see that they're gone."

"How do you know that they were staring at our apartment?"

"Because of the angle they were parked."

"What kind of car were they driving?"

"A black SUV."

"Did you see the license plates?"

"No, I didn't see it."

"Did you see how long they were sitting outside?"

"Maybe twenty minutes."

"If they were only sitting out there for twenty minutes, then they probably weren't the cops. Usually, when cops are squatting on you, they pull long hours. So those guys you saw might've been waiting on somebody."

"Nah, Zo, I know when I see a cop. And those guys definitely looked like cops."

"Well, I can't argue with you about that. Just call me if they come back."

"Okay," she said, and then changed the subject. "Can I get some money from the shoe box?"

"How much you talking?"

"Two grand. I wanna buy a YSL bag for the comedy show next weekend."

"Yeah, a'ight. Go ahead. But don't take more than that."

"I won't. And thanks, baby."

"You're welcome," I told her, and then I said, "Before you go, let me tell you what happened earlier today."

"What?"

"Well, I found out that Tim has been having an affair with Alayna. So I went to his office to approach him about it, and I burst into his office door and found one of the firefighters sucking him off."

"No fucking way!" Pricilla commented, sounding surprised.

"Yes way."

"So you caught them in the act?"

"Yes, homeboy was on his knees and Tim was standing up in front of him. The shit fucked my head up."

"What did they say?"

"What could they say? The dude serving Tim was looking stupid in the face. And the only thing Tim could say was 'Leave my office.'"

"Did Alayna see it?"

"She was behind me, so she didn't see them in action. I'm kind of glad she was, because she would not have been able to handle it."

"Damn! So Tim banging dudes now?"

"It appears that way."

"So, did you get a chance to check him about Alayna?"

"Not at that moment. I did step to him later, after I calmed down."

"What did you say to him?"

"I just told him that he violated the code when he started fucking with my sister. I mean, come on, baby, the guy is old enough to be her father."

"Yeah, I know. But did you say anything to him about his extracurricular activities?"

"Not until later."

"So, where do you and he stand now?"

"I honestly don't even know. It's like I don't even know him anymore."

"So, does this interfere with the business arrangement you two have?"

"Not that I know of. But it wouldn't surprise me if he tells me he doesn't want in anymore."

"If he tells you that, will you stop doing it?"

"Remember we stopped before."

"Yeah, but when shit started getting tight for him, y'all started it back up. So, my question to you is, if he comes to you and say the same thing again, will you stop?"

"Nah, I'm not stopping. I'm gonna do it as long as I can. We've got bills and a wedding to pay for."

"Yes, we do, and I forgot to tell you that I invited five more people. So I'm gonna have to call our wedding planner and let her know that."

"Cilla, don't invite any more people. We've already went over the initial budget. Cut me some slack."

"Okay, baby. I won't invite any more people. And if this makes any difference, the five people I invited are cousins on my daddy side."

"I don't care who they are. No more invites."

"Okay . . . okay . . . I heard you loud and clear."

"Well, let me get off this phone. I love you."

"I love you too, baby. Be safe if you get an emergency call before morning."

"I will."

CHAPTER 12

Alayna

WHEN I WOKE UP THIS MORNING, I FELT LIKE SHIT. THERE WAS like a black cloud looming over my head, and at that point, I knew I couldn't be around this place any longer, so I called my husband. After I got Levi on the phone, I asked him to come and pick me up. He arrived about an hour later. The only person I said goodbye to was Alonzo. He was on his way out of the station himself, to run an errand, he said. Other than that, I was off and looking forward to the next few days away from this place.

In the car, Levi sparked up a conversation. "Are you okay? Because your mood seems off a little."

"Yes, I'm fine. But I am a little tired."

"Think you might be pregnant?" he asked with optimism.

"No, silly. I just got my period a couple of weeks ago."

"But that was two to three weeks ago."

"Leave it alone. I am not pregnant."

"Did you hear about that old man from Lake Edward getting murdered and robbed?"

"So, wait, the cops are saying it's a murder and robbery now? Because when Zo and I saw it on the news, they said that the man might've died from a heart attack. And when they reported that, they didn't mention any money."

"Well, now they classified it as a murder, and the daughter said that her father kept a lot of money in his fireproof safe and that now it's missing."

"Damn, that's fucked up. I know she's seriously hurt to have found out that. Did they say they had any suspects?"

"No suspect yet. But one of the neighbors said that they saw a car in the driveway of the old man's house, around the time the murder happened. But they can't give a good description because it was getting dark out."

"Well, I hope they find the bastard, because you can't just go around robbing people and killing them. What nerve!" I commented.

While Levi and I talked about the unfortunate situation, his cell phone rang. He looked at the caller ID and said, "It's my mama. Hold on. Hello."

I couldn't hear what she was saying, but I pretty much figured out what they were talking about when he said that he'd stop by the pharmacy and bring it to her. When he ended the call, I looked at him and said, "She wants you to pick up a prescription for her, huh?"

He gave me a goofy-ass facial expression. "Yeah, how did you know?"

"Because you said that you were going to stop at the pharmacy. And you know I hate stopping at a lot of places before I go home. Can you please drop me off first?"

"But it's on our way."

I sucked my teeth. "You always do that."

"Do what?"

"Every time your mother calls, you drop everything and fly over there. And now you're holding me up from going straight home because she wants you to stop by the pharmacy. She has a car, why can't she do it herself?"

"What is it with you and my mother? You act like you hate her."

"I don't hate her. She's just annoying at times. And every time she tells you to jump, you say how high."

"That is not true."

"Yes, it is, and I am tired of it." Then I said, "When is your car getting fixed? When did they tell you it would be ready?"

"They said that I needed a new transmission."

"And how much is that?"

"Thirty-five hundred."

"And when did you find out about that?"

"A few days ago."

"And you're just now telling me."

"I knew you were going to hit the roof, that's why I didn't tell you."

"So, if you knew this, days ago, why would you try to buy your mother a one-thousand-dollar painting for Mother's Day? Does that even make sense to you? Because it sure doesn't make any sense to me."

"I figured that if I bought her the gift, she'd loan me the money for my car."

"And what if she doesn't?"

"Then I don't know."

"You need to see someone, Levi, because your thought process is off."

"There you go, being disrespectful. How would you feel if I told you something like that?"

"I'd feel nothing, because you would never."

"Now see, that's the shit I be talking about. You have no regard for me whatsoever. Sometimes I feel like I'm in this relationship alone."

"I can make it a reality."

"See, there you go again. You sure know how to be a bitch sometimes."

Hearing the word "bitch" sent me into a fit of rage, and without even thinking twice about it, I backhanded Levi and hit him in his mouth. *WHAM!*

"Owww!" he said, and then cradled his mouth with his hand. "What the fuck did you do that for?" he griped.

"That's for calling me a bitch!" I roared. "Don't you dare talk to me like that!" I was seething at the mouth. There was nothing that would make me extremely angry until you called me a bitch. That word was so degrading to me. It tells a woman that you have no respect for them. "Take me home right now. I don't even want to see your mother," I ordered him.

I thought he was going to give me some pushback, but he didn't. He took the next exit and drove me straight home. I got out of the Jeep without saying a word to him and went into the house. When I got inside, I looked out the window to see what he was doing; he had pulled away and left. I yanked the curtain closed and said, "I bet you won't talk to me like that again."

I felt the need to get in the tub and take a long, hot bath. Maybe it would relax me a little and ease my mind from all the chaos that transpired yesterday. I swear, for the life of me, I couldn't wrap my mind around the fact that Tim and I were done. My heart ached for that man who didn't deserve me, and after finding out that he was now involved with another man, why should I care? What was wrong with me? Was I sick in the head? Or was I desperate to be loved by the wrong man? Either way, I knew I was dealing with a serious case of low self-esteem. And if I didn't find a way to rid myself of it, my life would take a nosedive into a bucket of shit before all was said and done.

Too bad I couldn't have this conversation with my brother. He had zero tolerance for issues like this. Throughout my entire life, his only advice to me was to let "shit roll off your shoulders and keep it moving." But it had never been that simple. For him, it had been. I was the type of person where I wore my heart on my sleeve. And when somebody bothered me, the whole world knew. Hopefully, one day, I could change that. But until then, pray for me!

CHAPTER 13

Tim

I WANTED TO SAY GOODBYE TO ALAYNA BEFORE SHE LEFT THE STATION, but when I looked in her room and found out that she was gone, I figured that it was too late. She must've gotten out of here before sunrise. "Did you see what time Alayna left this morning?" I asked Paul when I entered the kitchen. He was sitting down eating a bowl of oatmeal when I walked in. He was always the first one up in the morning. If anyone knew what was going on around here, it would be Paul.

"No, I haven't seen her at all. Is everything all right?"

"Yeah, everything is cool," I told him, and headed outside the station.

When I stepped outside, I noticed that no one was out there, and I noticed that Alonzo's car was gone. He didn't tell me that he was leaving either. I could only hope he was out there taking care of business and not getting into any trouble. I didn't want to believe it, but my gut told me that he had something to do with that old man's death. I could only pray to God that he didn't. But something wasn't adding up with me.

I grabbed my cell phone from my back pocket and dialed Alayna's number. I stood next to the fire truck and listened to the line ring. It rang five times and then went to voicemail. I knew Alayna like the back of my hand. She had her phone in her hand, looking at me calling her, but refusing to answer it. So I dialed her number again and listened to it ring. This time, she answered on the third ring.

"Hello," she said.

"I appreciate you answering the phone," I told her. I honestly didn't think that she would answer it.

"What do you want, Tim?"

"I wanted to see you before you left this morning."

"For what? What difference would it have made?"

"I wanted to say goodbye, since I wasn't going to see you for a few days."

"You know what? I've decided not to come back. I'm gonna take some time for myself and then I'm gonna go into another field of work."

"Why?" I asked her. What was she thinking?

"It's just time for a change."

"But you liked it here."

"Yeah, I did, before all that drama unfolded," she said, and then paused. "Tim, I can't walk around there and pretend that everything is hunky-dory with us. For God's sake, my brother caught Jesse giving you head. Do you think that I can walk around there, knowing that you and Jesse had something going on too? I can't be around that."

"What if I get rid of him? Will you come back then?"

"No, Tim. I'm done. I'm gonna take this break, reflect on my life, and then I'm gonna do something else."

"You hate me, don't you?"

"No, Tim, I don't hate you. I'm disappointed."

"Well, let me assure you that this won't change the arrangement we have. I'll still make deposits in your bank account. That is, until you find another job."

"No, I'm good. The money you've given me over the past year and a half is enough for me to live off, until I find another gig."

"Are you sure?"

"Yes, Tim, I'm sure." She then fell silent.

"Have you talked to your brother since you left? Does he know that you're not coming back to the station?"

"I've talked to him. But I haven't told him that I was leaving for good."

"When did you talk to him?"

"When I was leaving this morning. He walked out of the station the same time I did."

"Did he say where he was going?"

"No, he didn't. Why? Is there something wrong?"

"I'm just a little concerned about him and the way he's been moving these last couple of weeks."

"If you're talking about how he reacted toward you and Jesse—"

I cut her off. "No, I'm not talking about last night. Did you hear about the young lady finding her father dead on the floor of their house?"

"Yeah, we both saw it on the news last night. Why?"

"I think he may have been involved."

Alayna burst into laughter. "Wait, you think my brother killed that man?"

"I don't think he did it deliberately. I believe that he went there, asked the old man for the money he owed him, the man refused to give it up, and Zo hit 'em."

"Okay, now you're reaching."

"How is that?"

"Why would he owe my brother money?"

"Are you naïve? Where do you think all this money I'm giving you is coming from?"

"Your paycheck."

"Wake up, Alayna, your brother and I only make eight-five thousand a year. And Kirsten is a stay-at-home mom, so I pay the mortgage, car notes, and every bill in the home. So all that money is gone. If we weren't getting the kickbacks from the homeowners' insurance policies, we'd be in the red."

"For some reason, I thought y'all stopped it."

"Yeah, we did for a couple of months. But stuff got tight again and we had to pick that hustle back up."

"Well, I still don't believe that Zo had anything to do with that man's death. I know my brother and he won't hurt a fly."

"You don't know your brother like I do. He's a hothead and I've had to check him on many occasions. I don't know what he's got going on in his personal life, but whatever it is, it's making his tolerance level very low."

"I think he's still mourning over our father's death."

"How are things at home with his girlfriend? Are they in a good place?"

"I haven't heard anything."

"Well, just keep a watch on him. And please don't tell him that we had this conversation."

"For the sake of keeping the drama down, I won't tell him. But make this the last time you call me."

"Damn! You're cutting me off for good?"

"I'll tell you what—don't call me. I'll call you when I'm ready. Deal?"

I hesitated for a second and then I agreed. "Deal."

After I got off the phone with Alayna, I sat there and reflected on the conversation I had just had with her. She ended our call with such finality. Was she really done with me? Was our relationship over? If that was the case, then I knew that I truly screwed up. If I had been more careful about my relationship with Jesse, I'd still be able to be with Alayna. I knew I would miss her dearly, because she brought something special to our relationship. And I would not be able to get that special certain thing from Jesse or my wife, so it looked like I would have to go without it. Damn!

After mulling over all the things I would miss by not being with Alayna anymore, I decided to call Alonzo. He answered on the second ring.

"What's up, boss man?" he shouted through the phone. I could tell that he was driving around town with his car windows down.

"Where are you?" I asked him.

"I'm out doing a pickup."

"How long will you be?"

"Not long. After I'm done, I've gotta make a quick trip home. So I should be back within the hour."

"Keep your nose clean."

Alonzo chuckled. "What does that mean?"

"It means, keep your nose clean," I repeated.

"Yeah, a'ight. See you when I get back." He ended the call.

As badly as I wanted to reiterate my suspicions concerning his involvement with the murder, I held my tongue for several reasons. One, we were on a city-monitored phone, and two, I didn't want to create more tension between us than there already was. I figured it was best to let this thing play out naturally. Besides, if there was a chance someone was listening in on our call, I wouldn't want them to link me to that dead man. That would open a can of worms and I couldn't have that. No way! Got too much to lose. If Alonzo fell, he would do it alone.

CHAPTER 14

Alonzo

THIS MORNING RUN WASN'T GOING TO TAKE LONG, BECAUSE THE couple knew I was coming and they knew how much to give me. When I knocked on their door, the wife answered. Her name was Beatrice Nichols; her husband was Arthur. They were an older couple—I would say in their midsixties. They had a lot of fire damage to their garage, back patio, and the third bedroom on the right side of the house. I can't say what they got in an insurance payout, but I knew with the report we wrote, they came off with at least two hundred thousand dollars. All Tim and I asked for was thirty thousand. They agreed to give it to us, so now I was here to collect.

"Hi there, young man," she greeted me.

I smiled. "How are you?"

"Good, come on in." She stood to the side so I could walk by her.

"I can't stay long. Gotta get back to the station before an emergency call comes through and the crew needs an extra hand," I shared as I crossed the threshold of the doorway.

"It's okay. We won't keep you long. Arthur is in the kitchen, so follow me," Mrs. Nichols said after she closed the front door and led the way. I followed her to the kitchen, which was only a couple of feet from the front door. When I entered the kitchen, Mr.

Nichols was sitting at the table, eating and drinking a cup of coffee. I walked toward him and shook his hand. "Good morning," he said.

"Good morning to you, sir."

"Have a seat and take off your gloves. Beatrice, pour him a cup of coffee."

"No, I'm good. I just came by to get the check and then be on my way."

"Beatrice, hand him that check on the countertop, over there by the toaster oven." Mr. Nichols pointed.

Mrs. Nichols grabbed a loose check and then handed it to Mr. Nichols. He, in turn, handed the check to me. I immediately looked down at the check after I got it in my hand and I wasn't at all pleased with what I saw. The fucking check was written for ten thousand dollars. Not the thirty we agreed to. "This is wrong."

"What do you mean it's wrong?" Mr. Nichols asked.

"Who wrote this check?" I wanted to know.

"My wife wrote it."

"Well, she wrote the wrong amount."

"And how is it wrong?"

"We agreed to thirty thousand."

"See, that's the thing, son. After my wife and I talked about it, we came to the decision that that was too much. You'd be robbing us if we gave you that much money. What you did for us was only worth ten thousand dollars, so that's what we're giving you," he explained.

"Do you realize that if we didn't write the report the way we did, you wouldn't have gotten as much as you did?"

"Son, I understand where you're going with this, but with all the repairs and things we did, we can only give you ten thousand dollars."

"First of all, stop calling me 'son,'" I snapped. My voice ricocheted around the walls of the kitchen as I roared. My facial expression was that of a madman who was about to rip some things apart.

Mr. Nichols stood up. "You better lower your voice in my house. Now you better be lucky that we're giving you that. Somebody else would probably give you nothing!" he roared back.

"So you're not giving me the thirty thousand you and your wife agreed to?" I asked him. But I said it in a way that got him to think about what he was saying to me. Meanwhile, I was sizing up him and his wife. Trying to figure out if they were the type of people that would call the cops if I threatened to kill them if they didn't give me the money that they had promised. I needed the money. Not the heat. And if they called the cops on me, I could forget about the thirty grand and this ten-thousand-dollar check in my hand.

"You better take that check in your hand and get the hell out of my house before I change my mind about giving you that," he warned me.

Without giving it any thought, I shoved the check down into my front pants pocket, rushed over to Mrs. Nichols, grabbed her by the hair, and yanked her toward me. The two-hundred-pound Florida Evans look-alike screamed and stumbled a bit as I dragged her to the area of the kitchen where the knives were and I snatched one out. I held it to her neck and started making my demands. "Get the fucking checkbook out and write me a thirty-thousand-dollar check or I'm gonna slice this bitch's throat! Do you hear me?" I roared at him.

He threw up his hands. "Okay . . . okay . . . I will get you another check. Just don't hurt her."

I held the knife tightly in my hand, and just at the right angle against Mrs. Nichols's throat, while she whined and begged me not to kill her. "If your husband gives me what I came here for, then I won't kill you."

"Arthur, please give him the check." She pleaded with her husband.

"I'm getting it . . . I'm getting it . . ." he announced as he grabbed a pen and checkbook from the kitchen drawer filled with envelopes and bill statements. He stood there with both items in his hands and looked at me. "She normally writes out the checks."

"Wait, you don't know how to write a check?" I screamed at the old man.

"My wife normally does it. She knows where to put all the information," he explained.

I sucked my teeth and thought for a moment. And then it came to me. "Put the checkbook and the pen on the countertop and sit down. And, Mrs. Nichols, we're gonna walk slowly over to the countertop so you can fill out the check. Now if you make a sudden move, I'm gonna cut your fucking throat. Do you understand?"

"Yes, I understand," she whimpered.

"Look, shut the fuck up with all that crying. You're driving me nuts with it," I scolded her.

"Okay . . ." she said, and tried silencing her cry. She was about to fall to pieces.

"Now let's move slowly," I told her, and then we started making steps toward the countertop where the checkbook was. It took us about five complete steps to get to it. Mr. Nichols watched us the entire way.

As soon as we reached the checkbook, Mrs. Nichols grabbed the pen and began to fill out the check; I still had the knife angled against her neck. I loosened my grip just a tad bit so she could stand straight up and write it. "I'm writing this check out to you?" she asked me.

"No. Write it out to Alayna Curry."

"How do you spell that?" she wanted to know.

"*A-l-a-y-n-a* . . . Curry," I told her.

"And this is for twenty thousand?"

"No. Write it for thirty thousand," I growled at her.

"But we already gave you a check for ten," she reminded me.

"That check will be for my troubles. Now write thirty thousand in the amount section."

As instructed, Mrs. Nichols wrote the check for thirty thousand, and when she tore the check from the book, she elbowed me in the stomach and tried to escape from the clutches of my arms and the knife, but my reaction didn't bode well with sudden movement. The blade from the knife in my hand cut through the first layer of skin around her neck and then it went deeper. The blood from her neck squirted out like a busted water pipe and I let her go. She staggered around the kitchen, making gurgling sounds with her mouth and holding her neck with both of her hands, but it wasn't enough pressure to hold off the amount of blood she was losing. Mr. Nichols jumped up from his chair, grabbed a dish towel, rushed to his wife's aid, and tried to add pressure to her wound, but blood kept gushing. There was so much blood on the floor that Mrs. Nichols ended up losing her balance and tumbling on the floor. Mr. Nichols fell down on his knees and began to cradle her in his arms. Within a blink of an eye, Mrs. Nichols stopped breathing.

"Oh, no, you killed my wife!" he started shouting as he rocked her back and forth in his arms.

"If you guys would've done what we agreed upon, this wouldn't have happened," I pointed out.

"Fuck you, you little punk! You think you're a fucking murderer and a thief! Preying on honest and hardworking people like us. Do you think that you're going to get away with this?" he continued to shout.

"Yeah, I do," I told him, and then I got behind him and slit his throat wide open. Blood started gushing out of his neck and then he slumped over on his wife's body.

I stood there and looked at the entire kitchen. The whole scene was bloody. And as I glanced around, surveying the area, my eyes landed on the check Mrs. Nichols wrote for the thirty thousand dollars. It was on the countertop, near a sugar canister, and from where I was standing, there was not a drop of blood on it. So I tiptoed over there, making sure that I didn't step in any of the blood, and I took off my right glove, because I didn't know if I had gotten any of the Nichols blood on it. I grabbed the check, folded it in half, placed it in my front pocket, and then I carefully made my way out of the kitchen. Before I exited the house, I put the glove back on my hand, and I looked out the windows of the front room to make sure no one was around. And when I felt like the coast was clear, I made my way out of the house. I kept my head down as I walked to my car. Before I opened the driver's-side door, I took off both gloves and held them in my hand. Once again, I didn't want to get any of the couple's blood in or on my car. After I climbed inside, I kept my head low and drove out of there slowly and quietly so that I wouldn't bring any attention to myself.

I drove nine miles before pulling my car over to the side of the road. And when I got out, I tossed the gloves in a curbside sewer. "Won't catch me with bloody gloves," I said, and then I got back inside my car. As soon as I sped off, I headed to Alayna's house. I wanted to hurry up and give her the check so that she could deposit it before the cops found out that the Nicholses were dead. On my way there, I couldn't help but think about what I had just done. Killing that couple wasn't what I had planned to do. All I wanted was the money that was owed to me. That's it. And if they would've given it to me, they wouldn't be dead right now. So, in essence, it was their fault, because I'd always been a pretty fair guy. It was not in my nature to go around and hurt people. So just give me what's mine and everything would be cool. Stop fucking playing games with me or I would be forced to continue to act out this way.

Alayna's house was only fifteen miles away, so it only took me about twelve minutes to get there. She was in her living room watching TV when I knocked on the front door. "What brings you by?" she asked after she let me in and closed the door behind us.

I grabbed the thirty-thousand-dollar check from my pocket, held it in the palm of my hand, and then I sat down on the smoke-gray sectional she had just bought for her place. She sat down two feet away from me. "I stopped by to bring you this check so that you could deposit it in your account," I informed her, and handed her the check.

She opened it and looked at it. Her eyes lit up. "This is a thirty-thousand-dollar check."

"Yeah, I know. Deposit it. And when it clears, give me twenty back and you keep the ten."

"Who are Beatrice and Arthur Nichols?"

"A couple that I did the paperwork for on their insurance claim."

"I knew that. But they got it like this to give up thirty stacks?"

"That's what we agreed upon. They got back over two hundred K."

"Oh, okay. Now that makes sense."

"Make sure you go and deposit it today. I don't want them to change their minds and try to stop payment on the check."

"So I get to keep ten of it?"

"Yep."

Alayna got excited. "Wooo-hooo! I'm gonna go out and treat me to something really nice," she said.

"Good. 'Cause you deserve it. Well, let me go. I've gotta stop off to my crib before I head back to the station," I announced, and stood up from the sofa. Alayna stood up too.

"So, how's the wedding planning going?"

"Let's just say that Pricilla is breaking the bank."

"Now don't let her put you in the poorhouse."

"I won't," I told her as I began to walk to the front door.

"I decided that today was the last day at the station," she said, changing the subject.

I stopped at the front door and turned around and looked at her. "You're quitting?"

"I've already quit. With that drama going on there, I don't want to be around it, so I'm done."

"Does Tim know this?"

"Yeah, he called me because he said that I didn't say goodbye this morning when I left. And I told him then."

"And what did he say?"

"Nothing really. He acted like he understood."

"Wow! That's surprising."

"I know."

"Are you sure you really wanna do that? Remember you said that you wanted to carry on Dad's legacy?"

"Yeah, I know. But I'm officially done. I mean, who knows? Maybe I could change my mind six months from now. Maybe even in a year. But for right now, I'm done."

I let out a long sigh. "Well, okay . . . if you say so. Just do what makes you happy."

"And that's exactly what I am doing."

"Good. Then it's settled," I said, and then I made my exit.

CHAPTER 15

Alayna

I KNOW ZO WANTED ME TO DEPOSIT THE CHECK YESTERDAY, BUT AFTER lying on the sofa and watching TV all day, I became restless and didn't want to leave the house. I did, however, get my butt up this morning and made the drive to Wells Fargo, but not before stopping by Pricilla's home first. I wanted to borrow a Gucci bag she just purchased not too long ago and kept forgetting to pick it up from her. She was on the phone talking when I let myself into her apartment. I could tell that she was talking to one of her homegirls.

"We're getting fitted this weekend, so try to lose some weight by then," she told the caller, and I burst into laughter. There was one thing you could count on: Pricilla would embarrass you without feeling bad about doing it. She was a very straightforward and blunt person. She never held back her feelings and would embarrass someone quick. But for some reason, she'd never tried to embarrass me. I guess it was because she knew that she'd be barking up the wrong tree. Or maybe it was because she knew how my brother was about me, and he was not going to tolerate it.

I couldn't hear what the caller was saying, but whatever it was, Pricilla wasn't bothered by it and quickly ended the call. "Girl, my sister-in-law just walked in. I'll call you back later."

As soon as she disconnected the call, she burst into laughter too. "Who was that?" I wondered aloud.

"My friend Pat. Every time I get on the phone with her, she always chewing on something. I told her that if she keeps gaining weight, she's not gonna be in my wedding. I can't have fat girls walking down the aisle before me. My bridesmaids have to represent. Remember we gotta take pictures too."

"Oh, Pat's not that bad. But she could stand to step back from the table a few times a day," I commented, then chuckled.

"What brings you by?"

"Do you remember you said that I could borrow your Gucci bag?"

"Oh, yeah, be right back," she told me, and tried to leave me in the living room.

"Oh, no, you ain't leaving me. I'm coming to see what else you got in that closet back there," I insisted.

Pricilla was a label ho. Every designer bag that came in style, my brother made sure she had it. That's probably where all his money was going, in addition to the wedding they're planning.

When I reached Pricilla's bedroom, she was already in her walk-in closet, so I followed her inside. It felt like I was in a Neiman Marcus department store. She had expensive handbags and shoes everywhere. If I could wear her shoe size, I would borrow some of her shoes too.

"Here you go," she said, and handed me a bag.

"What do you mean, 'here you go'? Are you giving this to me?" I asked.

"Yes, I am."

"No way," I said, and examined the signature Gucci *G*'s that were emblazoned all over the bag. Even the buckle was gold plated. I hugged her. "Thank you so much."

"You're welcome. Now lets get out of here before you start looking at my other bags," she commented, then escorted me out of her closet and bedroom. When we reached the living room, I plopped down on the sofa and admired my bag some more.

"Girl, I wasn't expecting this."

"Well, consider it a gift. You're like the best sister-in-law that a woman could have," Pricilla told me, and sat down on the sofa next to me.

I reached over and hugged her again. "You're the best!" I mentioned.

"Thank you. But are you ready for the wedding? Because I'm about to pull my hair out. It's so much stuff to do."

"Don't you have a wedding planner?"

"Yes, but I've still gotta check up behind her. I've wanted to fire her so many times, but your brother insists that I don't."

"Yeah, he's right. Just let her do her job. I'll pitch in if you like."

"Nah, I'm good. You just keep looking fabulous. And maybe my bridesmaids would follow suit."

"How is your mother?" I asked.

"She's good. She's always worrying me to death about how much money I'm spending."

"Maybe she's just concerned."

"No, she's not. She's just mad because my dad only gave her one hundred dollars and told her to do with it what she pleased."

"Oh, that's cold."

Pricilla laughed. "I know."

"So, how long is it going to take you and my brother to have a baby? You know I need a niece or nephew."

"Girl, your brother tries to put a baby up in me every chance he gets. It'll happen. So, will you be able to go with us to the fitting this weekend?"

"Yeah, I don't see why not."

"Too bad Levi doesn't want to be in the wedding. It would've been nice if he could be one of the groomsmen."

"He's such a party pooper. He acts like he's the one that gets his cycle every month. And not me," I said, laughing.

"Ahh . . . leave him alone. He's a nice guy."

"Yeah, until he starts bitching!"

"Just give him a break. He'll get it together."

"If he doesn't, I'm gonna replace him."

Pricilla gave me a high five. "I know that's right," she commented.

She and I talked for at least another twenty minutes, until I told her that I had to leave and make a run to the bank. I didn't tell her about the check Alonzo had given me the day before. I figured that if he wanted her to know about it, then he'd tell her on his own. I stay out of husband-and-wife business. I've got my own shit to deal with at home with Levi.

The lobby of the bank wasn't packed, so I was happy about that. I wanted to get in and get out. When it was my time to perform my transaction with the teller, I greeted the older, Caucasian woman with blond hair and handed her the check addressed to me with the amount of thirty thousand dollars on it. She looked at the check and asked me for two forms of ID. I handed her my driver's license and bank debit card.

"I'm only trying to deposit it," I told her.

"Sure, I can take care of that." She started keying information into her computer. She stood there for a second, frozen like she was reading something, and then she asked me to excuse her. With my IDs and check in hand, she walked away from her teller station and disappeared into a back room. She returned about five minutes later with one of the bank managers. He was a middle-aged Black gentleman dressed in a bargain-basement suit. He kind of reminded me of the actor and comedian Wayne Brady from *Let's Make a Deal*. He introduced himself and immediately asked me to meet him at the door six feet away to my right and that he'd be on the other side to let me in.

"Why do I have to go to that door?" I asked him.

"Because I am going to take over this transaction," he informed me.

"But all I'm doing is depositing it. So, why do I need you to do that?" I wanted to know. He wasn't making any sense to me.

"Mrs. Curry, will you please meet me at that door?"

"What's behind that door?"

"My office."

"This isn't going to take long, is it? I've got other errands to run."

"No, ma'am, this won't take long at all."

I took a deep breath, exhaled, and then I proceeded to the door. As soon as I approached it, the bank manager opened it and let me in. His office wasn't directly behind the door. We had to travel down a hallway and around a corner. After walking about twenty yards, we finally made it to his office.

"Take a seat," he insisted.

So I sat down in one of the two chairs placed in front of his desk, while he sat down in the chair behind his desk.

"This isn't going to take long, is it?" I wanted reassurance.

"No, ma'am, it isn't," he told me, and placed my driver's ID and debit card in front of him. He placed the check on the keyboard and had it leaning against the computer monitor. "So you know Mr. and Mrs. Nichols?"

"Yes."

"How long have you been knowing them?"

"What's with the questions?"

"I'm just making conversation."

"Well, I'm not in the mood to conversate. If I would've known that it was going to take this long to deposit a check, then I would've gone to another branch."

"This would've happened there too."

"But I deposited a fifteen-thousand-dollar check last week and I didn't have to go through this."

"That's because this checking account was flagged. That's all."

"Who flagged it?" I asked. I was curious to know. Alonzo just gave me this check last night.

"Looks like there was a stop payment on it," he replied.

"That can't be right."

"Well, that's what my system is telling me," he said as he looked at the computer monitor.

I stood up from my chair and reached for the monitor so I could turn it around toward me. "Let me see."

He blocked my hand. "I'm sorry, but I can't let you look at this customer's account information."

"So, what am I going to do now? I provided them with a service and they need to pay me," I complained.

"Let me see if I can get them on the line. Maybe they can straighten this whole thing out," he said, and then he picked up the phone. But before he could dial the number, someone knocked on the door. He got up and opened it. On the other side of the door, a woman and a man, both dressed in suit jackets and slacks, with gold badges pinned in full view on the waist area of their pants, stood there. They introduced themselves as federal agents. Shook his hands and then all three of them turned their attention toward me. I sat there in full panic mode because I was trying to figure out why they were here. And they didn't take long to tell me. The woman introduced herself as Special Agent McGee, shook my hand, and introduced her male partner as Special Agent Fletcher. The bank manager handed them my ID and bank card, took a seat back behind his desk, and watched them as they began to interrogate me.

"I'm sure you know why we're here," the female agent started off saying.

"No, I don't. But I'm sure you're about to tell me," I said.

"This check you're in possession of is stolen."

"Well, I didn't steal the check."

"Where did you get it from?"

"I got it from them."

"When? Because they're dead."

"Dead!" I shouted, shocked by this statement.

"Yes, they're both dead. So, when did they give you this check?" she pressured me. She looked at me, dead-on. It seemed as though she could literally see right through me. But before I answered her question, I needed more information on the couple.

"How did they die?" I turned the question back on her.

"We were hoping you'd tell us."

"But I don't know, which is why I'm asking you."

"Cut the shit, Alayna, and tell us what you know," the other agent chimed in.

Taken aback by his outburst, I turned toward him. "But I don't know shit."

"This is a thirty-thousand-dollar check. Why would this couple give you that type of money?"

"Because I do interior decorating and I gave them a consultation. That check in your hands is the deposit for the job."

"So you're an interior designer and you did a consultation with this couple and they agreed to pay you thirty thousand dollars?"

"Yes, they did."

"Didn't you used to work as a firefighter?"

"Yes, I did."

"And were you on location when they had a fire some months back?"

"Yes."

"Did you know them before the fire?"

"No."

"So, when did you start the interior design business?" Agent McGee pressed.

"Maybe a month ago."

"Did you get a license for this business?"

Frustrated by all the questions, I snapped, "What does a business license have to do with anything?"

"I need to know if you have a legitimate business or not."

"Well, I reserve the right to remain silent. If you want any more answers out of me, then contact my lawyer," I told her. I wasn't going to let her trick me into answering questions and later have her find out that what I said was a lie. No way.

"Alayna, when did they give you the check? Do you have receipts to prove that you were employed by them?"

"I told you, I reserve the right to remain silent."

"Are you covering for someone? Because if you are, we can help you. Just tell us when you got the check."

"All I can say is that the check isn't stolen. It's their handwriting."

"Whose handwriting is it?"

Stunned by the question, I didn't know whether to say the husband or the wife. Before I put my foot in my mouth, I thought it was best that I keep my mouth closed. "I'm done talking."

"Alayna, we're investigating a series of robberies and murders, involving insurance scams. Now if you want to be pulled in this and take the fall, we'll start the paperwork. But just know that you'll never see the light of day. You will spend the rest of your life in federal prison. Is that how you want to spend the rest of your life?" she asked me, and all eyes were on me.

I couldn't believe that I was sitting in the bank manager's office talking to federal agents about a check I was trying to deposit into my account, along with money I already had sitting in there. Could I really get locked up for the rest of my life? To hear the words "will spend the rest of your life in federal prison" evoked a different kind of reaction inside me. I'd seen Court TV and the reactions of men and women after they got sentenced to lengthy prison terms. I'd also heard so many horror stories about doing prison time with other inmates that are dangerous and will kill you for a fucking honey bun, or to prove a point, and that wasn't my idea of how I wanted to live out the rest of my life. I wanted to have kids and watch them grow up, go off to college, and have families of their own.

Sitting here in this chair, surrounded by federal officers, was not the ticket. All I had to do was tell them that Alonzo gave me the check, but then where would that leave him? I'd be ratting my brother out and that went against everything that I believed in. I was taught as a child that family stuck together. Never let anyone come between us. Our father embedded that in our family's heads. Zo lived by those same values. So I refused to let any agent come between that.

"Excuse me, Agents. But am I under arrest?"

Both agents looked at one another. And then they turned their attention toward me. "No, you're not," the female federal agent replied.

I stood up and walked toward the door of the bank manager's office.

"You know that if you walk out of here, there's no coming back," the female federal agent commented.

"Say no more," I told her, and then exited the office. The agents watched as the door closed shut.

I knew that I looked confident leaving the bank manager's office, but I was scared out of my mind. But before I walked completely out of the bank, I grabbed my debit card and driver's license from the bank manager and told him good day.

As soon as I got into my Jeep, I powered it on and drove away from the bank. Thank God he answered on the third ring.

"What's up?" he answered.

"We need to talk."

"What happened?"

"I was just at the bank with the check you gave me, and the bank manger called federal agents," I said, and then paused.

"Alayna, I told you to deposit the check yesterday. Why didn't you listen to me?"

"I'm sorry, but I got tired and figured that if I held on to it for another day, it wouldn't hurt."

"What did the Feds say?"

"They tried to get me to answer a whole bunch of questions."

"Okay. Don't say another word. Go home and I'll meet you there," he instructed me.

"Will do," I assured him, and then I ended the call.

It only took me ten minutes to get home, so I was shocked to see that Zo had gotten there before me. I climbed out of my Jeep and met him on the sidewalk of my house. "So, what did they say?" he asked, getting straight to the point.

"They wanted to know if I knew the person who wrote me the check, and I told them, of course, and how would I have had the check if we didn't know each other? And then they asked me why was the check for thirty thousand? And I told them that I did interior decorating and consultation on the side and I provided them a service and this was what I charged them."

"That was a damn good answer. And what did they say?"

"They asked me if I had the documents to back up that I had this business and a copy of the receipt I gave to the couple."

"And what did you tell them?"

"I told them to get it from my lawyer, and if I wasn't under arrest, then I was out of there."

"Did they say that you were under arrest?"

"I'm standing right here in front of you, right?"

Alonzo burst into laughter. "Yeah, you sure are." He hugged me. "I'm proud of you. You did a good job."

"Answer this one question for me." I turned the questions to him.

"What's up?"

"Is that couple really dead?"

"I don't know. I haven't heard anything about it."

"Are you sure? Zo, you know you can tell me anything. Be straight up with me. You know I got your back."

"Baby sis, if I knew, I would've told you by now. You know I've always been straight with you."

"Okay. Well, be careful, because Tim thinks you're involved somehow with these people dying."

"Did he tell you that?"

"Yeah, he did. But I laughed it off, because I know you. You wouldn't harm a fly."

"Where was I when he said that?"

"He called me the morning after I left the station. Remember you were leaving the same time I was leaving?"

Perplexed by what he was just now hearing from Alayna, Alonzo looked over his shoulders in both directions and then looked in the direction of his car.

"Whatcha thinking about?" I asked him.

"I can't believe that son of a bitch said that to you behind my back. So I'm wondering if he told somebody else that bullshit!"

"If he knows like we know, he'd keep his mouth shut. He's got as much to lose as you do."

"My thoughts exactly," Zo agreed, and then he leaned over and kissed me on the cheek. "I'm gonna call you later," he said, and then he jogged back to his car. I watched him as he climbed inside and drove away.

As I made my way into my house, my cell phone started ringing. I pulled my phone from my purse and noticed that it was Levi calling me. I wasn't in the mood to talk to him, so I tossed my phone back in my purse. But immediately after it stopped ringing, it started ringing again. By this time, I was unlocking the front door of my house and walking in. After I closed the door, I reached back in my purse and grabbed my phone and saw that it was Levi calling once more. I reluctantly answered it. But I sighed first.

"Hello."

"Do you know that I am at the freaking grocery store and the debit card isn't working?"

"What are you talking about, it's not working?"

"I'm in the self-checkout lane and I used the card and it was declined. So I logged into our account and it won't allow me to see what we have in the account. The screen says to call your financial institution. So, can you please tell me what's going on?"

"I just left the bank and everything was fine," I told him, and then it dawned on me. Did the Feds put a freeze on my account? Alarmed by the thought of it, I told Levi to use another card.

"But I don't have another card. I maxed out my credit card to get my car fixed."

"Well, then, just leave the stuff there. I'll call you back," I said, and then I ended the call. At that very moment, I felt anxiety consume me. What if it was true and the Feds froze my account? How the fuck would I operate on a day-to-day basis?

"Okay, Alayna, calm down. You're overreacting. Just call the bank and see what's going on," I said out loud, giving myself a pep talk while I grabbed my debit card from my wallet and dialed the 800-number that was listed on the back of the card. As soon as I was connected to the automated system, I used the right button prompts and waited for a customer service rep to pick up. After waiting for what seemed like forever, I finally heard a male voice.

"Thanks for calling Wells Fargo, how can I be of service to you?" he asked. I went straight into explaining mode. So, once I answered all the security questions, he broke the news to me that my account was indeed frozen and that he couldn't tell me anything else about it. I sat there on my sofa in shock. But then I went into panic mode. What was I going to do?

"Wait, I gotta call Zo. He'll know what I need to do," I said aloud. So I dialed his number. He answered my call on the first ring.

"What's up, sis?"

"The Feds froze my bank account."

"How do you know that?"

"Because Levi called me and told me that he was at the store and his debit card was declined. So I called the bank and they told me that my account was frozen."

"How do you know that the Feds did it?"

"Because I just know. Who else would do it?."

"A'ight, don't worry. We'll figure something out."

"What am I going to do about money? I have my life savings in that account."

"I'll bring by some money later. So just calm down."

"What am I going to tell Levi when he asks me why is our account frozen?"

"I don't know. Tell 'em anything. Tell 'em you owe someone and they put a lien on your account."

"I have A-1 credit, Zo. He's not gonna believe that."

"Well, shit! Just make something up. And I'll stop by later."

"Okay," I said, and then we ended the call.

For the first time in my life, I felt uneasy about my brother's actions. I have always lived by the saying "I am my brother's keeper." But was I in over my head this time? Had I bitten off more than I could chew? I knew one thing: I had some stuff to figure out and I now realized that I didn't have much time to do it.

CHAPTER 16

Tim

I WAS IN MY OFFICE FILLING OUT ANOTHER FIRE INSPECTION DOCU-
ment when someone knocked on my office door. I stood up
from my chair and opened it. To my surprise, there were two
federal agents standing at my door. I can't lie and say that my
heart didn't leap from my chest, because it did. But I knew that
I had to play things cool and find out why they were here.

"Good day," I said, sounding calm, cool, and collected.

The woman extended her hand and introduced herself as
Special Agent McGee, and her partner introduced himself as
Special Agent Fletcher. "May we come in?" she asked.

"Oh, sure," I said, and opened the door wider so that they'd
have room to walk into my office. "Have a seat."

While they were taking a seat, I sat back down in the chair behind my desk. I saw Agent McGee scan my desk with her eyes,
trying to read what I had written on the documents scattered
across my desk. But I quickly gathered them up, to prevent her
from seeing what I had going on.

"What brings you guys here?" I wondered aloud.

"We're investigating a murder of an older couple that wrote a
check to Alayna Curry for thirty thousand dollars. And we're
here hoping that you could answer a few questions for us."

Shocked by Agent McGee's admission, I sat there not knowing whether or not I should help them by answering whatever questions they had, or telling them to piss off. Now I figured that if I told them to piss off, they'd assume that I was uncooperative and might drag me into this mess.

"So, can you tell me the name of this older couple?" I questioned them first.

"Mr. and Mrs. Nichols. They were murdered in their kitchen yesterday morning. Both of their throats were slit from ear to ear. Today, Alayna Curry tried to deposit a thirty-thousand-dollar check written out to her. The bank manager at Wells Fargo called us because there was a freeze activated on their account. When we asked her, why would they write her a check for that much, she told me that she did some interior designing for them. We're not sure if that's true or not, but what we do know is that she works here as a volunteer firefighter."

"She used to work here," I corrected them.

"Can you tell us when was her last day?"

"She put in her two weeks' notice a couple weeks ago," I lied. "But her last day was yesterday."

"Do you remember putting out a fire for them a couple of months ago?"

"Vaguely."

"Does the Shore Drive neighborhood ring a bell?"

"You're talking about a couple months ago. We've been in that neighborhood at least five times since then," I told her.

She pulled a photo of the couple from the inside of her jacket pocket and placed it onto my desk. I picked it up and looked at it. Truthfully, I didn't have to look at the picture. I had already known who these people were. I also knew that Alonzo was going to pick up a thirty-thousand-dollar check from them. But the fact that the check was written out to Alayna threw me for a loop.

"Do you remember this couple?" she asked me.

"Yes, I remember meeting them," I replied, and handed the photo back to her.

She took it from my hand and placed it back inside her jacket pocket. "Do you think that Alayna is capable of killing them?"

"Of course not. She's harmless."

"What about her husband, Levi?"

"I don't know much about him."

"But if you have to guess off the top of your head, would you say that he's capable of doing something like that?"

"Again, I don't know much about him."

"So you're not saying either way?" she pressed.

"No, I'm not saying anything, because I've never really been in his company."

"What about her brother, Alonzo Riddick? I understand that he works here too?"

"Oh, no, he's a gentle giant," I quickly said.

"Is he here today? We would love to have a word with him."

"No, he's not here. He ran out to run a few errands. But if you leave your card, I'll make sure he gets it," I assured the agent.

"Sure, I can do that." She reached in her pocket, grabbed her business card, and handed it to me. I took it, placed it inside the top drawer of my desk, and then I stood up from my chair. "I appreciate you stopping by . . ." I stated, letting them know that I was ready for them to leave.

They caught the hint and stood up too. "And we appreciate your time," she replied, and then they both walked toward my office door.

I beat them there and opened the door. "Thanks for stopping by," I told them.

"Don't mention it," Agent McGee responded nonchalantly as they both exited my office.

I watched them walk down the hallway toward the station's exit door, and when they walked through it, I let out a long sigh as I closed my door.

I grabbed my cell phone from the holster attached to my belt and dialed Alonzo's number. Thankfully, he answered on the first ring.

"What's up?" he asked.

"You need to head back to the station."

"Do we have an emergency?"

"It's worse than that," I told him.

"I'm on my way," he assured me.

CHAPTER 17

Alonzo

I HAD NO IDEA WHY TIM HAD CALLED ME, BUT IT SOUNDED SERIOUS. Come to think of it, it sounded like he'd probably talked to Alayna. Or he'd seen something else on the news. Either way, my mind told me to make a trip to the bank, so I stopped and grabbed nine-thousand dollars in cash and headed back to the station. While en route, I called Pricilla.

"Hey, baby," she said cheerfully.

"Hey, listen . . . I need you to go to the bank and withdraw nine grand in cash. And then I want you to get a cashier's check for the rest of what we got and make it out to yourself."

"Is everything all right?" She seemed concerned.

"Yes, everything is fine. Just do it now and I'll call you later."

"Okay," she agreed, and then I ended the call.

I arrived at the station about fifteen minutes later. When I got there, I went straight to Tim's office. I passed Jesse on the way. He had a stupid-looking expression on his face, but I refused to entertain him and kept moving. I knocked on Tim's door and he invited me to come in.

"What's going on?" I asked while standing in the middle of his office floor.

"Two federal agents just stopped by here asking questions

about Alayna and a thirty-thousand-dollar check written out to her from a fucking dead couple. Can you please tell me what's going on? And why was the check written out to her?"

"You said that they were dead?" I tried to act surprised. There was no way I could let on that I knew about that couple's demise. If I did, he'd know that I had something to do with their death. I was sure he suspected me because of that old man in Lake Edward suffering the same fate.

"Yeah, they're dead, and it's not looking good for us. And especially for Alayna."

"What did the agents say?"

"I've already told you what they said. Now you tell me why the thirty-thousand-dollar check was written out to Alayna?"

"Because I told them to, that's why."

"But why bring her into this?"

"I just thought that if the check was written out to her, it wouldn't bring the unwanted attention to us."

"Well, that didn't work," Tim informed me, and then he went inside his top drawer, grabbed a business card, and held it out for me to take.

"What's this?" I wanted to know as I reached out and grabbed it.

"One of the agents' business card. She left a couple for us. Said that she wanted you to give her a call."

"Yeah, a'ight, let's see how long she waits on it," I commented, tore the card in half, and dropped it in Tim's trash can.

"Do you think it's a coincidence that three people we got money from was found murdered in their homes?"

"So, what are you saying, Tim?" I asked defensively, because I knew where he was going with this.

"Did you have anything to do with those people dying?"

"No, I didn't."

"Alonzo, you know you can be honest with me. Your secret would be safe with me."

That's what he was telling me, but I didn't believe him. Tim was different now. It seemed like ever since I caught him in that compromising situation with Jesse, I didn't know him anymore. I guess he could probably say the same about me. But there was no way that I was going to tell him that I murdered those people. Was he out of his fucking mind? That would be just like signing my own prison sentence, and I wasn't ready to go to prison. I got shit out here in the free world to do. Getting married to my fiancée was one, and I couldn't do that behind bars.

"There's no secret to keep safe. You know that I wouldn't kill anybody," I said as sincerely as I knew how. It was important to get Tim to believe me; this way, he wouldn't get scared and try to rat me out.

"Are you being up front and honest with me?"

"Come on now, Tim. You know I am." I tried reassuring him.

He looked at me kind of sideways, searching my face for any type of deception. And when I didn't change my expression, he exhaled and said, "Okay. I believe you, but we've gotta do a few things different. If another person we're dealing with dies, the cops are going to suspect foul play."

"What do you suggest we do?"

"I want you to lay low. Let me pick the money up from the next few pickups, while you hang around the station."

"All right, sounds good to me." I didn't put up a fight. I figured he wanted to take control of the operation and I was fine with it. Yeah, let him get his hands dirty, once and for all. Let him get a taste of those homeowners trying to scam us out of what's rightfully ours. He'd see what I had to deal with these past couple of days. "Is that it?" I wanted to know, because I got tired of standing around in his office. I was beginning to feel like I was closed off in there.

"Yeah, that about sums it up. Do you have any questions for me?"

"No, I'm good."

"Okay. Well, I guess that's it."

"All right. Well, I'll be in my room if you need me."

"Copy that," he said, and then I exited his office.

But for some reason, after I left, I felt an uneasy feeling about Tim. I felt like he was holding back something from me. Had he already ratted me out to the Feds? Damn, I sure hoped not, because if he did, he was going to regret the day he met me.

* * *

As soon as I walked in my room, I got Alayna on the phone. "You're not going to believe it."

"Believe what?"

"The same two federal agents that you saw at the bank stopped by here and asked Tim a bunch of questions about you and I."

"What did they say?"

"They pretty much asked him the same questions they asked you. How did you know the Nicholses, and why was the check for thirty thousand dollars? They even wanted to know if you were still working here."

"Did Tim tell them that I quit?"

"Yeah, he told them."

"So, what happens now? Are they gonna try to pin that murder on me?"

"What murder?" I heard a voice say in Alayna's background, and I instantly knew that it was Levi.

"Is Levi there?"

"Yes, he just walked in the house."

"Who are you talking to on the phone?" Levi's tone got louder. "And who was murdered?" His questions continued.

"Let me call you back," she said.

"Okay, but don't tell him anything about what's going on and what we talked about," I instructed her.

"Okay," she replied, and then we ended the call.

I sat there on my bed and thought about Pricilla. After knowing what I now knew, I needed to find out if she went to the bank, like I told her to. So I immediately dialed her number. Her phone rang six times before she answered it; this infuriated me.

"Hello," she finally said.

"Why did it take you so long to answer your phone?" I went in on her.

"Because I was trying to get back in my car, when my phone started ringing."

"But you always have it in your hands."

"Well, I had it in my purse this time. And why are you yelling at me?"

"I got a lot on my mind. Where are you?"

"I just left the bank."

"So you got the cash and the cashier's check?"

"Yes, I do."

"Good girl. Do me a favor and take all the cash to Alayna. And when you get home, put the cashier's check in the safe."

"Okay, but is everything all right?"

"Yes, everything is fine," I assured her.

"You aren't lying to me, are you?"

"I'll explain everything to you in due time," I promised her. "Look, I've gotta get off this phone. Don't forget to go to Alayna's house and give her that money."

"I'm gonna head over there now."

"Okay, good. I love you."

"I love you too," she told me.

Immediately after I got her off the phone, I exited my room, went into the supply closet near the truck port, and grabbed a screwdriver from the toolbox. When I had it in hand, I went back to my room and unscrewed the filter vent in my room and hid all the cash I had behind the filter; then I screwed the vent back in place. That was officially my new hiding spot, just in case there was an emergency and I couldn't get to my other stash.

CHAPTER 18

Alayna

"**W**HO WAS THAT ON THE PHONE?" LEVI WOULDN'T LET UP AS he stood there in the middle of the floor of our living room. He had just come home from work, so I knew that there was no escaping him.

"It was Alonzo," I finally told him, going directly against what my brother had told me to do.

"Why would someone want to pin a murder on you?"

"No one is pinning a murder on me."

"Well, who was murdered?"

"An old couple that I did some work for." I continued to explain it to Levi, even though I knew I should've kept my mouth closed.

"They've got names, don't they?"

"Mr. and Mrs. Nichols."

"And what kind of work did you do for them?" Levi kept pressing the issue.

"Their house caught on fire a few months back, and before they got their house repaired, I gave them some pointers and advice on fireproofing their home," I told him, knowing half of what I was saying was a lie. But I couldn't tell him everything.

"So, when were these people killed?"

"A couple of days ago, I think."

"So, how did Alonzo find out about the couple?"

"I guess he saw it on TV."

Levi stood there and looked at me sideways. "Well, if it was on the news, then how come we haven't seen it?"

"Have you been watching the news lately?"

"No."

"Then that's why."

"Did you find out why our bank account is frozen?"

"Yeah, I found out that there's a lien on it. Apparently, someone won a judgment against me a long time ago and recently slapped a lien on me."

"How much is it for?"

"Forty thousand dollars." I lied to him once more. I couldn't say a smaller amount, because if I did, he'd tell me to let the person have it so that the lien could be lifted, and we would have access to our account again.

"That's everything we've got in our account!" he roared. He was seething at the mouth.

"No shit!" I mocked him.

"So, what are we going to do?"

"Alonzo said that he's going to spot us some money until we can remedy this situation."

KNOCK! KNOCK! KNOCK! Levi and I turned our attention toward the front door. "Who is it?" he asked.

"It's Pricilla." Alonzo's fiancée's voice shouted from the other side of the door.

Levi walked to the front door, opened it, and let Pricilla in. She was smiling from ear to ear when she entered my apartment. She hugged Levi first, then walked over to the sofa, leaned toward me, and hugged me too. After she released me, she sat down next to me.

"I'm gonna leave you two alone," Levi announced, and then he headed to the back of the apartment. I heard the bathroom door close, so I knew he was in the bathroom. That's when I turned my attention toward Pricilla.

She reached in her purse, grabbed a wad of money, and handed it to me. "Your brother told me to bring this to you."

My eyes lit up. "Oh, thank you, girl!"

"It's nine grand," she told me.

"You just don't know how much this is going to help me," I replied.

"Is everything all right?"

"Something unexpected popped up on us. But we're gonna be fine," I assured her. I figured that my brother hadn't filled her in on what was going on, because if he did, she wouldn't be questioning me. "So, how is the wedding planning going?" I changed the subject while stuffing the money she gave me underneath my thigh. I didn't want Levi to see it, if he decided to return to the living room. I also didn't want to let on that I had just seen Pricilla at her apartment not too long ago. I pretended like I hadn't seen her in a while, and she went right along with it.

"It's going well. I just invited five more people, and your brother is not at all happy about it."

"You must've gone over the budget?"

"I did. But I assured him that I wasn't gonna invite anyone else."

"Is your dress done?"

"Almost. I go to my last fitting in three weeks."

"You don't look like you've gained any weight."

"Thank God! But I did change the design a little, so that's why I have another fitting. After that, the design will be complete. Time seems like it is going by so fast. I mean, I'm getting married in less than eight weeks!"

"Yes, you are. You're going to be Mrs. Alonzo Riddick."

Pricilla's face beamed like a princess's. "Yes, I am, and I can't wait!" Then she looked down at her watch. "I've gotta get out of here. I'm meeting my sister for lunch, and I'm gonna do some retail therapy. Your brother said that I could buy me a purse to take with me to the comedy show next weekend," she added as she stood up and walked toward the front door.

"Must be nice," I commented, and stood up behind her. I reached back and grabbed the money from the sofa and then I stuffed it down into my pocket.

"Oh, it is," she said as she opened the front door.

"Drive safe out there," I told her as I made my way to the front door.

"I will," she assured me, and turned her back to leave. I watched her until she got out of sight and then I closed the front door.

It seemed like as soon as she left, Levi reappeared. "What did she want?"

"She just came by to check on me."

"She didn't stay long."

"That's because she said she had to meet her sister for a lunch date."

"You hungry?"

"Kind of, why?"

"Because I was going to go in the kitchen and make a couple of turkey and cheese sandwiches."

"That sounds good. But let me tell you what I did after you dropped me off this morning."

"I'm listening."

"I quit the station."

"You quit?"

"Yep, I no longer work as a volunteer firefighter."

"No way, are you serious?" Levi said with a little cheerfulness.

"You sound so happy."

"That's because I am. Now I don't have to worry about if you and Tim are messing around with each other anymore."

"Baby, that whole situation is dead."

"Good, I'm glad. But tell me," he added.

"What?"

"Does she know about the affair?"

"Who?"

"Pricilla?"

"Of course not," I lied to him. I didn't want him to think that he was the laughingstock of our marriage.

"Are you telling me the truth?"

"Of course, I am. That's not for her to know."

"Okay. If you say so," he said, and then he left the room. I heard him chuckle on the way out. I guess he found the whole situation funny. I, on the other hand, didn't, because I was affected by it. If only he knew the whole true. Instead of laughing on the way out of here, he would've been crying and asking me why.

CHAPTER 19

Tim

I WAS IN THE STATION'S KITCHEN, SITTING AT THE TABLE SIFTING THROUGH a car magazine and eating an apple, when one of my firefighters, Paul, walked in from the truck port. He had just finished restocking the inside of the paramedic cab. "I'm sure gonna miss Alayna restocking the ambulance," he commented as he grabbed a bottle of water from the refrigerator.

"Yeah, she was a major source of help around here," I replied after taking my attention from the magazine in my hand.

Paul sat down at the table across from me. "Is it true that you were hitting that?" He chuckled and gave me a wink. "Lucky man!"

I gave him the evil eye. "Come on now, Paul, let's not do that."

Paul took a sip of water from the bottle. "Okay, my bad! Off limits."

"Tell me, who's spreading lies around here?"

"I'm swearing to secrecy," he added, and then he smiled in a grimace-type way.

"I'm sure you do."

"What do you think about these older people being murdered? Isn't it weird that they were all fire victims?" Paul asked.

I swear, that question came from out of nowhere, and yet, this had been on my mind since I'd seen it on television. But I didn't know how to respond to it. I had suspected that Alonzo was be-

hind it, but I couldn't tell Paul that. That would open the floodgates of questions about why Alonzo was dealing with those people in the first place. Thankfully, my cell phone rang before I
was stuck with having to answer his question. I held up my
pointer finger to indicate that I wanted him to pause that question so I could answer my phone.

"Hello," I said.

"Hey, buddy, this is Bobby."

"Hey, Bobby, what can I help you with?"

"I was just talking to some buddies of mine about going on a
fishing trip and I thought about you. Think you'd be interested
in going?"

"Who's all going?"

"Rick, he's the vice mayor of Norfolk."

"I think I've met him before."

"Yeah, and then there's Pete. He's the lieutenant at my
precinct. My partner, Max, may tag along, but he's gotta see if
he could take off."

"When are you guys planning to go?"

"In a couple of weeks."

I thought for a second. "Yeah, I could manage and swing
that."

"Great. Then it's settled. I'll call you back in a few days and
confirm everything to you."

"Hey Bobby, wait . . . I wanna run something by you," I said,
and then I got up from the table. I left the kitchen of the station
altogether and headed in the direction of my office, because I
didn't want Paul eavesdropping on my conversation. When I got
halfway there, I said, "Hey, have you heard about those elderly
people murdered in Virginia Beach?"

"Yeah, I know one of the detectives working on the case with
the old man that lived in Lake Edward, why?"

"What if I told you I may know something about that case?"

"Are you saying you know who committed the murder?"

"Let's just say I may have a hunch."

"I'm all ears."

"But, wait, how can I cover myself and make sure I don't get burned if my suspicion is true?"

"Do you have a hand in the murder?"

"No."

"Then you can't get burned."

"But let's say that I was involved in something else, and that something else caused the old man's demise?"

"In that case, you would need immunity. So my advice to you is to get with an attorney, map out your options, and then sit down with the detective and tell him what you know. If you want, I could get that detective on the line. He's a reasonable guy."

Instantly feeling flustered and pressured, I declined Bobby's offer. "Let me think about it first and then I'll let you know."

"Okay, well, don't wait too late. Don't wanna read about you in the newspaper, friend."

I chuckled, trying to downplay my role in this whole mess. "Trust me, I'm not connected in that way," I assured him.

"Awesome, because you had me nervous there for a minute. Well, you have my number. Call me if you need me."

"I sure will," I said, and then I ended the call.

After I hung up with Bobby, I wondered, had I blown my own cover by telling him what I'd known? I also wondered if he was going to think that I was more involved than what I let on. Out of all the years I'd known Bobby, he'd always been a tough cookie to figure out. Always wore a poker face when you needed to read his thoughts. All I could say was that I hoped I didn't mess myself up with that open dialogue I just gave him. And let me add, I would pay a lot of money to know what he was thinking about right now.

CHAPTER 20

Alonzo

FINALLY I HAD A DAY OFF. BUT MY FIRST DAY OFF FOR THE WEEK HAD to be spent at the bakery for a cake tasting. My fiancée would've gone nuts if I changed my mind at the last minute and decided not to come. So here we were at this bakery in Norfolk, tasting different flavors and fillings to go inside of our wedding cake. The owner of the shop was Kim Newsome. She was a popular young white woman, with pink, blue, and blond hair, and tons of baking experience, I'm told. She came highly recommended, as far as the tastes of her desserts. But her prices were out of this world. Pricilla, her sister, Yona, their mother, and I sat at a round table with the owner of the bakery, who was sitting across from us. She brought out a variety of mini cake bites with different-flavored jams and fillings we could add to our wedding cake. I was instantly sold on the yellow cake filled with the strawberry jam.

"This is the one I want," I told Pricilla and Kim.

Kim smiled.

"But you haven't tasted the other cake bites," Pricilla pointed out.

"I don't need to taste the other ones. I want this." I pointed to the rest of the cake bite left on my plate.

"Baby, just try the chocolate cake with the chocolate ganache."

"Yes, please do. And while you're doing that, we have the vanilla cake with passion fruit. This is our coconut Key lime cake with cream cheese icing. Then we have Victorian wedding cake, which is a buttercream frosting and raspberry jam within the layers. Here's our carrot cake with buttercream frosting. And, lastly, we have this Prosecco-infused cake filled with a fresh, ripe peach buttercream," Kim explained.

There were a lot of cakes to choose from, because after we tasted everything, they were all good. I figured I'd play the backseat role and let Pricilla choose which one she wanted. With her mouth filled with the Victorian cake, she pointed toward her mouth and gave us a head nod.

"Well, then, that settles it. She likes the Victorian cake," I announced.

"Seems that way to me too," Pricilla's mom agreed.

When Pricilla was about to comment, five people came walking through the front door of the bakery and we all turned our attention toward them. As soon as I zoomed in on the group of people, I realized that they were federal agents and Norfolk city police officers. The woman in the group approached me and said, "Alonzo Riddick, you are under arrest for the murder of Mr. and Mrs. Arthur Nichols, so please stand up."

"Wait, there must be some mistake. I ain't killed nobody!"

"Yeah, he didn't kill nobody, lady!" Pricilla jumped to my defense.

"Well, the evidence we have against you says you did. Now stand up!"

Dumbfounded, I stood up from my chair and turned around so I could be handcuffed. Pricilla, her mother, and her sister all started asking the agents and the cops questions about who I supposedly murdered, and how they couldn't just barge up in here and arrest me like this. But they could. I was guilty as hell. But my question was, how did they link me to that couple? Where in the hell did I go wrong? I was careful not to leave any fingerprints on the scene or get any blood on me. Did one of the neighbors see me? Or did Tim rat me out? I knew one thing, if Tim had something to do with my arrest, I would make sure that he was dealt with. Swiftly.

As the cops and the agents escorted me out of the bakery, the bakery owner stood there in disbelief while I heard Pricilla in the background assuring me that she was going to get me out of this jam. "I'm gonna call our lawyer right now!" But what lawyer was she talking about? We didn't have a lawyer. So, was she saying it to let the agents know that we had an attorney on speed dial? I knew one thing, it sure sounded good.

"Call my sister and let her know what's going on!" I shouted.

"Okay. I'm gonna call her now," Pricilla assured me.

"Don't worry, she's going to be in a jail cell next to you when we're done," the female agent said.

I looked into her face and smiled. But I refused to utter one word to her. By smiling, I wanted her to know that what she was doing wasn't fazing me one bit. And with the right attorney, I was gonna blow this case.

I watched Pricilla and her family go toe-to-toe with one of the cops. I couldn't hear what they were saying, but they were not happy. That much I can say.

"Where am I going? To the Norfolk City Jail?" I asked the city cop who would drive the patrol car.

"No, we're just an escort. I'm taking you to the federal building," he said. "Is it true that you killed that elderly couple?"

"Nah, don't believe everything you hear," I advised him.

"Trust me, I don't," he replied.

While sitting in the back of the squad car, I could see the sheer embarrassment on Pricilla's face as she defended me to the agents. The female agent handed a card to her, and I could tell that my fiancée was mortified. I couldn't read her sister or mother's face, but I could tell that they were in as much shock as Pricilla was. Their mom tried to remain calm, but seeing her daughter in despair did a number on her.

After sitting there in the car for about fifteen minutes, the cop finally got in the driver's seat and drove away. I was glad that he had, because I couldn't stand seeing my future wife in so much pain. I swear, I wished I could snap my fingers and make this whole thing go away. But since I couldn't, I just figured that I'd put an *H* on my chest and handle this situation head-on. That was all I could do at this point.

CHAPTER 21

Alayna

"Y<small>OUR CELL PHONE IS RINGING!</small>" L<small>EVI SHOUTED FROM THE LIVING</small> room.

"It's probably Alonzo. Answer it!" I shouted back from the bathroom. I had just gotten out of the shower and I was in there drying off with a towel.

"No, the call is coming from Pricilla!" he yelled back.

"See what she wants."

"Hello," I heard Levi say, and then he fell silent. Seconds later, he said, "Okay, hold on, Pricilla."

"What did she say?" I yelled from the bathroom.

"She wants to talk to you," he informed me from the other side of the door.

I opened the bathroom door and took my cell phone from his hand. I wrapped the towel around me and placed the phone up to my ear. "Hey, girl, what's up?" I asked her.

"The police just arrested Alonzo, and I need you to meet me down at the federal building."

Instantly filled with anxiety, I tried to collect my thoughts, because my mind started jumping all over the place. "Wait, when did this happen?"

"A few minutes ago. We were at our cake tasting and two plainclothes agents, along with three Norfolk city cops, walked inside the bakery and told him that he was under arrest."

"Did they say why they were arresting him?"

"For murder. They said that he murdered two old people."

"Where are you now?"

"I'm standing outside the bakery."

"Get in your car and meet me down at the federal building in forty-five minutes."

"Okay, see you then," she said, and then we ended the call.

I opened the bathroom door and noticed that Levi was standing there eavesdropping. "What was that all about?"

"Why are you being nosey?"

"I wanna know what's going on, Alayna."

"If you must know, Alonzo was arrested in Norfolk, and I'm gonna meet Pricilla down at the federal building to find out what's going on."

"Why was he taken to a federal building? Shouldn't they have taken him to a regular jail?"

"I'll find that out when I get there," I told him. I already knew why they took him to a federal building, but Levi didn't need to know why.

"Do you need me to go with you for moral support?"

"No, I've got this." I figured the less he knew about this situation, the better off all of us would be.

It didn't take me long to get dressed. I was out of my apartment in less than twenty-five minutes after I hung up with Pricilla. My heart raced the entire drive to the federal building in Norfolk. After I arrived in the area, I founded a parking space about a quarter of a mile away and had to walk the rest of the way. Pricilla's car was nowhere in sight, so I took it upon myself to go into the federal building, with the hopes that I would find her there. When I was approached by one of the U.S. Marshals, I asked about Pricilla and her family, and he told me that no person matching Pricilla's, her mother's, or her sister's description had come in the building. He added that I had to make an appointment with the arresting federal officer, so I had no other option but to exit the building.

On my way out, I walked into Pricilla and her family. Pricilla cried loudly when she saw me. I embraced her and she broke down into tears. I held her tightly in my arms and gave her permission to cry.

"They got Alonzo, Alayna. What am I going to do?" she cried out, her words were somewhat muffled as she buried her face in my chest.

I massaged her back. "We're gonna get him out, so don't you worry," I promised her.

"You just came from out of there, right?" Pricilla's mother asked me.

"Yes, ma'am."

"What did they say?" her sister added.

Pricilla lifted her head away from my chest, wiped away the tears from her eyes with the back of her hands, and waited for me to answer.

"I spoke with a U.S. Marshal and he told me that we've gotta make an appointment with the federal agent that arrested him."

"Are you freaking kidding me?" Pricilla's mother spat.

"Yeah, are they crazy?" Yona asked.

"That's what he told me."

"Who did you talk to? What's his name?" Pricilla wanted to know.

"I didn't get his name. But he's the only white man standing by the front door," I told her.

"Well, I'm going on to see what he's talking about."

"I'm gonna go in with you," her mother insisted as she and Yona followed Pricilla inside the building.

"Well, I'm gonna wait out here," I told them, because I knew that they weren't going to get anywhere with that man. He was gonna send them right back out that front lobby door.

I stood there for about three minutes, and what do you know? Pricilla, her mother, and Yona were being led out of the building by the same white man I spoke to a few minutes before. And they weren't happy.

"I'm gonna find out who his supervisor is and report his butt, because he was nasty and disrespectful to me and my family."

"Yes, he was," her mother chimed in as she and Yona followed Pricilla down the concrete steps.

"What did he say?" I asked her.

"He basically told me the same thing he told you. That we can't see Alonzo, and if we want to get any information about his arrest, we need to contact the federal officer and make an appointment."

"Wait, he did say that an attorney would speed up this process," Yona reminded her.

"So, then, that's what we do," I agreed. "Do you know any good attorneys?" I asked Pricilla.

"Yeah, I know one. His name is Jeff Swartz. He represented my cousin on a murder charge some years ago," Pricilla explained.

"Did he beat the case?" I wanted to know.

"Yes, he did."

"Well, let's get him on the phone and make an appointment."

Pricilla, myself, Yona, and her mother stood around in a huddle as Pricilla looked up the attorney's name and phone number for his office. When she found it, she immediately dialed the number and placed the call on speakerphone.

"Thank you for calling Swartz, Goodlove, and Taliaferro Law Firm. This is Amanda speaking. How may I direct your call?"

"Is Jeff Swartz available?" Pricilla spoke into the phone.

"No, he's with a client right now. But if you give me your number, I could pass it along and have him call you back."

"I'm seeking his counsel, so I would like to make an appointment with him," Pricilla told her.

"Okay, what is your name?" Amanda wanted to know.

"My name is Pricilla, but it's my fiancé that needs representation."

"What is his name?"

"Alonzo Riddick."

"Is he in jail now?"

"He's being detained in federal custody."

"On what charge?"

"The federal agents that arrested him said that he murdered two people."

"How long has he been in their custody?"

"For about an hour and a half. And, see, I'm standing down here at the federal building now asking to see him or the agents that arrested him, and the U.S. Marshal told me that I had to make an appointment, which I thought was the stupidest thing ever."

Amanda chuckled. "Yeah, I know that seems weird, but that's their protocol. Okay, so I have a time slot open today for four thirty. Is that good for you?" Amanda continued.

"Yes, four thirty is fine," Pricilla replied.

"Okay, well, I guess we'll see you then."

"Thank you."

After Pricilla ended the call with Amanda, she stood there with the saddest facial expression. "Do you realize that our wedding is right around the corner?" she pointed out. "What if he doesn't get out in time?"

Her mother embraced her. "He will, honey."

"Yeah, we'll have him out way before then. You just gotta think positive," I chimed in.

"I guess you're right," she said.

"Have you spoken to Tim?" I asked Pricilla.

"No. You're the only one I talked to."

"Hold on, let me call him," I said, and then I pulled out my cell phone. I dialed Tim's cell phone and put the call on speaker.

"Hello," he said.

"Do you know that Zo was just arrested?" I didn't hesitate to say.

"No. I didn't. What was he arrested for?"

"Murder. The Feds arrested him inside the bakery where he and his fiancée was having their cake tasting an hour ago."

"Who did they say he murdered?"

"The older couple, the Nicholses."

"Oh, wow! That's not good," Tim responded nonchalantly.

"Did they talk to you after they came to your office the first time?"

"Who?"

"The Feds."

"No, I only talked to them that one time, and that was it."

"Well, me, his fiancée, and his future mother-in-law and sister-in-law are down here at the federal building trying to see him or talk to the federal agents, but the U.S. Marshals aren't letting us."

"Why not?"

"The white man said that we have to make an appointment first. So we called a lawyer, and if he's saying some good stuff, then we're gonna hire him to represent Alonzo and get him out of jail. Can't have him locked up when his wedding is around the corner."

"Yeah, that wouldn't be nice. Well, if you need anything, just call me," Tim insisted.

"Will do," I said, and then we ended the call.

"He didn't sound that concerned to me," Yona pointed out.

"I thought the same thing too," I said, agreeing with her.

"Zo told me that their relationship was changing," Pricilla stated.

"I witnessed that before I quit working at the station," I acknowledged.

"Wait, you quit?" Pricilla asked me. She was shocked.

"Yeah, I had to get out of there."

"Does Zo, know?" Pricilla's questions continued.

"Yeah, I told him."

"I wonder why he didn't tell me."

"Probably because it just happened a couple days ago. It may have slipped his mind."

"So, are you going to do something else?"

Before I could answer Pricilla's question, the door of the federal building opened and the white man peered his head around the door and said, "I'm sorry, but you can't hang outside this door."

"Are you kidding me right now?" I asked, turning around. He was a real jerk.

"No, I am not kidding," he replied.

"What is your problem, dude?" Pricilla asked him.

"Yeah, all we're doing is standing here and talking," Pricilla's mother interjected.

"I'm sorry, ladies. Those are the rules."

"Come on, you guys, before I say something and he have me arrested," I said, and grabbed Pricilla by the arms.

We complained to each other about the man's behavior toward us, until we got to the end of the block. There we switched gears and talked about the questions we were going to ask the attorney during the appointment. After we pretty much had a game plan in mind, we got into our cars and headed in the direction of the attorney's office. I drove ahead and Pricilla followed.

Once inside the office, we only had to wait fifteen minutes to see him. When he walked into the lobby and introduced himself, we got a full look at the distinguished white gentleman. He shook all of our hands and asked us to follow him to his office. After we entered his office, we all took a seat, one by one, and admired all the plaques and accolades he had placed on the walls and tables. Judging from those accolades, we felt we sure had picked the right person for the job.

"So, how can I help you ladies?" he started off saying.

Pricilla sat up in her chair. "Well, I'm here because my fiancé needs a lawyer."

"And his name is Alonzo Riddick, correct?" the attorney asked.

"Yes."

"So Amanda tells me that he was arrested for committing murder?" His questions continued.

"Yes, but he didn't do it." Pricilla didn't hesitate to defend him.

"Do you know the arresting officer's name?"

"I have one of their cards here," Pricilla told him, and then she handed him a business card she retrieved from her purse.

Attorney Swartz picked up the card and looked at it. "Oh, I know Special Agent McGee. She's a fair lady. I'll get her on the phone and find out what's going on."

"Oh, thank you, Jesus!" Pricilla's mother said aloud as she held her hands in the air.

"So, what happens next?"

"Well, I'm gonna give McGee a call. Find out exactly what he's being charged with. And then I'm going to see if I can get him a bond hearing—"

Pricilla cut him off in midsentence. "Please do, because we're getting married in seven weeks."

"Well, I can't make any guarantees. Federal laws are different from state laws. It's harder to get out on bond with federal charges pending. But it's not to say that it can't happen. It all depends on the charges and the judge," he explained.

"How much will this cost us? And how much is your retainer?" Pricilla wanted to know.

"My retainer is twenty-five thousand. My hourly rate for a murder charge is three hundred an hour."

"Damn, that's a lot of money," I chimed in.

"We're talking about murder charges, and it's being handled by federal officers. We're stepping into the big leagues. Normally, when you're indicted by a federal officer, it's because they have concrete evidence against you. And if that's the case, nine times out of ten, they will win their case."

"Well, we're the tenth of that example. Because I know my fiancé, he wouldn't harm anyone." Pricilla refuted that fact decisively.

"What does he do for a living?"

"He's a firefighter."

"For what city?" he asked while taking notes on a pad of paper.

"Virginia Beach. The Haygood location."

"And how long has he been a firefighter?"

"Seventeen years," I interjected.

"And who are you?" the attorney asked me.

"I'm his sister, Alayna. I used to work there as a volunteer. Our father used to be the chief there before he passed away some years ago."

"Is he involved in a charity?"

"Yes, on the board of the Children's Foundation of Scottsdale," Pricilla blurted out.

"I've heard of that nonprofit," Mr. Swartz acknowledged as he penciled that information down on his pad. "Okay, so here's what I propose to do. I will get on the phone with Agent McGee. Find out exactly what he's being charged with, see if there's a chance that he could get a bond, and then I'll file a motion for discovery."

"What is a motion for discovery?" Yona asked him.

"It's where the arresting officer has to show me the evidence they have and plan to use against Mr. Riddick."

"What if what they have on him is bogus? Will you ask the courts to drop the charges?" Pricilla asked.

"In some cases, that's likely. But again, we're dealing with an entirely different beast when we enter a federal court."

"So you're saying that it can't be done in federal court?" I chimed back in.

"No, I'm not saying that it can't be done, I'm only saying that it could be a challenge."

"Well, I heard you were the best, so we're gonna go with you," Pricilla told him.

"Well, that's good to hear. So, as soon as you come up with the retainer, I can start working on the case."

"Do you take cash?" Pricilla inquired.

"Why, yes, I do."

"Well, then, I shall be back," she told him, and then we all stood up.

We all shook his hand and exited his office. Outside, Pricilla's mother asked her about the retainer fee. "You have twenty-five thousand in cash?"

"Yes, Mommy, I do."

"In your house?" she wanted clarity.

"Yes."

"That type of money should be in the bank."

"It was, before I took it out a few days ago."

"You better be careful with that. If people knew that you had that type of money lying around, they'd try to break in your house and rob you."

"And that's why no one knew," Pricilla pointed out.

"Great point," I commented, and then I kissed all of them on their cheeks. "I'm gonna go back home. As soon as you hear something, call me," I instructed Pricilla.

"I sure will," she assured.

When I got into my car, I sat there for a moment and decided to get Tim on the phone. He and I needed to talk about this situation concerning my brother. I swear, I dreaded calling him because of what he and I were going through at this moment, but this conversation couldn't be brushed underneath the rug.

Surprisingly, when I called, he let the phone ring five times before he answered.

"Hello," he finally said.

"Did I catch you at a bad time? I mean, because you just hung up with Pricilla," I replied sarcastically. I was getting the vibe that he didn't want to talk to me, but changed his mind at the last minute.

"I had actually just come out of the bathroom."

I started to apologize for my intrusion, but then I hesitated after realizing who I was really talking to. This was the same man that cheated on me with another man, so why apologize to him for interrupting his bathroom break? What I needed to do was get to the point of why I called him.

"Hey, listen, what are we going to do about Alonzo?"

"What do you mean?"

"He's locked up, Tim! They have him in a jail cell pending murder charges."

"I know."

"Is that all you have to say? This is a serious matter."

"You're right, this is a serious matter, but let's not jump to conclusions. Let's allow this thing to play out and see where it takes him."

"I don't think that'll be a good idea. We've got to get in front of this. This is his life we're talking about."

"Remember that I questioned you about this situation right after it happened?"

"Yes."

"Do you see now why I brought it to your attention?"

"What are you saying?" Tim's words were gnawing at my curiosity.

"I'm not saying anything. Just keep your eyes and ears open, because it's about to get even more serious."

After Tim made his comments, the phone went radio silent, complete dead air.

"Hello," I said.

"Yeah, I'm here."

I exhaled after hearing his voice. "I thought you hung up."

"No, I was waiting for you to say something."

"I really don't know what to say. All of this seems so surreal. I mean, my brother is freaking locked up for something he didn't do."

"Are you sure about that?"

"Come on, Tim, you know Zo. He's just not that type of guy."

"That's the old Zo I know. This new guy that just surfaced a little over a week ago, I'm not too sure about."

"Tim, I don't appreciate your insinuation."

"Well, I don't know what else to say. Your brother's been on some other shit these past few days and I've been trying to reel him back in, but he's been giving me business. He won't listen to anything I have to say, so my hands are tied right now."

"So that's it? You're just gonna hang him out to dry?"

"No, I'm not saying that."

"Then what are you saying?" I asked him.

"I just think it's best to let his attorney handle it. If you guys get him the best attorney that money can buy, I believe he'll be in good shape."

I sucked my teeth. I knew Tim was blowing smoke up my ass. He was casually telling me that my brother was on his own—without actually telling me that. I'll give it to the son of a bitch; he was definitely good with wordplay. But he'd better be careful too, because if what he was saying was true about my brother, this whole thing with the insurance fraud was going to fall apart and it was going to affect him as well. So his nonchalant attitude had better change.

Once I figured I had heard enough from Tim, I ended the call. He wasn't saying anything I wanted to hear, in the first place. I disagreed when he said that my brother was a new guy—Tim was a new guy. He'd changed more ways than one, and I didn't like it.

CHAPTER 22

Tim

ALAYNA HAD A NERVE CALLING ME AND ASKING IF I SPOKE TO THE FBI agents after the first time they came to my office. What she failed to realize was that her brother was a stone-cold murderer and he was going to federal prison for a very long time after the judge got through with him. So her calling me and wondering what I was going to do to help him, or to come at me with the idea that she was gonna get some information out of me, was outlandish. My hands were tied and I wanted nothing to do with him or her. Good riddance to the both of them.

"Who was that on the phone?" my wife asked as she entered our bedroom. I was in the middle of getting dressed to go to the hat store.

"That was Alayna. She said that Alonzo was arrested earlier," I told her while I was putting on my socks.

"What was he arrested for?" Kirsten asked as she stood near our walk-in closet.

"Murder."

"Murder? Oh, my goodness! Who did he murder?"

"Do you remember seeing on the news about an older couple being murdered in their kitchen? They said that their necks were cut?"

"Yeah, I saw that a few days ago."

"Well, they're saying that Alonzo did it."

"Are you serious right now? Because those are some serious accusations."

"Yes, honey, I am serious right now."

"Do you think that he could do something like that?"

"I can't say." But what I really wanted to say was, of course, I do. Alonzo wasn't the same guy I used to know. This insurance scam we started went to his head and corrupted his mind.

"Well, I don't think he could. He just doesn't strike me as that kind of guy. He taught little T.J. how to throw and catch a baseball."

"I know, honey. But you can never know what a person is going through behind the scenes. People walk around with terrible thoughts in their heads and we'll never know about it until they do something like this."

"Well, I still don't think he's capable of doing something like that. They got the wrong guy," Kirsten said, and then she went into the closet.

"But what if he did do it?"

"Then he's going to pay a heavy price for it. You just can't go around and murder people and expect to get away with it," she added after sticking her head out of the closet.

"I guess we'll find out sooner rather than later," I said.

"We will, won't we?" she replied, and disappeared back into the closet.

"Someone was killed?" my son asked out of nowhere. There I was, sitting on my bed and putting on a pair of socks, and my son asked me and his mother, who was killed? Kirsten stormed out of the closet and raced to our bedroom door.

"See what I'm telling you, Tim. You can't talk around these kids. They hear everything."

"Who was killed?" he asked again.

"Someone on TV, son. Now go in your room."

"Yeah, get out of here, T.J. Grown folks were talking."

I watched my son as he hunched his shoulders and walked away from our bedroom door. "All I did was ask a question and I get chewed out for it," he said.

Kirsten stood at the entryway of our bedroom door and put

both of her hands on each side of her hips. "See, you gotta watch what you say around these kids. They're getting too grown for their own good."

"Well, then, stop talking about 'em," I replied, and brushed off the situation.

"I swear, these kids will put you in a grave early, if you let them," she observed, then walked back into the closet. I didn't say another word. Instead, I put on my shoes and exited the bedroom.

Before I could get out of the house, Kirsten tracked me down at the front door. "Tim, what store are you going to?" she asked as I walked down the front porch stairs.

"To the hat shop, why?"

"Because I need you to stop by the grocery store and pick up a few things, if you don't mind."

"But I do mind. I wanna leave this house for once and not have to run errands for you, Kirsten. This is my day off."

"You want to eat dinner, don't you?" she protested.

"Come on now, what kind of question is that?"

"It's a legitimate one."

"You already know the answer to it."

"Well, then, pick up a pack of ground beef and a can of tomato paste on your way back home. I'm making bake ziti tonight."

I shook my head with disgust. "She gets me every time," I said, and turned around and headed to my pickup truck. Once inside, I hurried up and sped away just in case she decided to get me to pick up another item. But while I drove, I realized that all she would have to do was either call or text me. So, what was the use?

CHAPTER 23

Alonzo

"WHEN WILL I BE ABLE TO GET MY PHONE CALL?" I ASKED ONE of the two U.S. Marshals, sitting at their desks, while I sat in a glass-encased cell. One of the marshals was a Michael B. Jordan look-alike and the other one kind of reminded me of the wrestler John Cena.

"You haven't gotten your call yet?" the John Cena look-alike asked.

"No."

The white marshal stood up and walked toward me. After he unlocked the door, he let me out and escorted me over to the phone station, ten feet away from the cell they had me locked in.

"You've got five minutes." Then he walked back to his desk, which was about ten feet away.

I knew I needed to call my fiancée. Thankfully, Pricilla answered her cell phone on the second ring. She sounded really happy when she heard my voice. "Are you all right, baby?" she asked.

"Yeah, I'm good. Sitting down here, waiting to see what they're going to do with me."

"Have they given you a bond?"

"No, all they've done was put me in a glass cell. I think I'm waiting for someone to come and talk to me. But I don't have anything to say to 'em."

"Good, because I spoke with a lawyer and I'm going to get him to represent you."

"What is his name?"

"Jeff Swartz. I heard he's one of the best."

"I'm sure he's one of the best, but does he specialize in federal cases?"

"Yes, he does."

"How much is he asking for?"

"He wants twenty-five thousand to retain him."

"Pricilla, that's a lot of money."

"That's not a lot of money when you're being charged with two murders."

"But I didn't do it."

"I know you didn't. But you're gonna need a good lawyer to convince the jurors of that. And besides, I need you home. We have a wedding date that's coming up."

"Pricilla, I can't think about that right now. I've gotta get out of this place."

"What do you think I'm trying to do?"

"Have you talked to my sister?" I changed the subject because it sounded like she was about to break down into tears. She does this when I'm not sensitive to her feelings.

"Yes, she went with me to the attorney's office."

"How does she feel about the attorney?"

"She said that she liked him."

"Twenty-five thousand is a lot of money to give that guy all at once."

"But we have it. And I need you home."

"All right. Give it to him. But make sure he knows that part of that money is to be used to get me a bail hearing."

"He knows that already."

"Did he say how long it would take to get me out?"

"No, we didn't discuss that. But I'm sure as soon as I give him that money, he's going to start making things happen."

"Okay, after you give him the money, ask him when am I going to see him."

"Don't worry. I'm on it, baby."

"Thank you."

"You're welcome," she said, and then she told me, "I love you."

"I love you too."

After I ended the call with Pricilla, I snuck and called my sister. I wanted to tell her where I had hidden money at the fire station, so that she could get it and hold on to it for me. The phone rang four times before she answered.

"Hello," she finally said.

I let out a long sigh. "Girl, I thought that you weren't going to answer."

"I was getting out of the car when my phone started ringing."

"I just spoke to Pricilla. She said you went with her to see a lawyer."

"Yeah, I did."

"What do you think about him?"

"He's high. But I think he'll do a good job for you."

"I told Pricilla to go ahead and give him the retainer. But I'm calling you because I want you to go by the station and get some money I hid behind the air filter in my room."

"How much is it?"

"Nine grand."

"What do you want me to do with it?"

"Just hold on to it, because I'm sure I'm gonna need it sooner, not later."

"Have you talked to the Feds yet?"

"No, not yet."

"Well, you know the lawyer isn't gonna want you to say something that would incriminate you."

"Yes, I know. I'm pretty much gonna let them do the talking," I informed her. "Have you spoken to Tim?"

"Yeah, I called him and told him what happened."

"What did he say?"

"He didn't say much."

"I'm starting to believe that he's the reason why I got arrested today."

"How could he do that?"

"Remember, they talked to him first."

"How can he influence them to arrest you?"

"I don't know. But I'm gonna find out."

"Well, I'm sure you are."

"Hey, it's time to hang up," the Caucasian U.S. Marshal told me.

"Who is that? A correctional officer talking to you?" Alayna wanted to know.

"No, that's one of the U.S. Marshals."

"Tell 'em he could be more polite."

"If I told him that, he'll try to throw his weight around. So I'm gonna hang up for now. But as soon as I talk to someone, I'll let you guys know what's going on."

"Okay, I love you."

"I love you too, sis."

The U.S. Marshal escorted me back to my cell, but as soon as I sat down, the same female and male FBI agent walked in and pulled me back out. I was then escorted to a room not far from the cell I was sitting in. The room was cold. It had one table and three chairs. The walls were blank. There was no two-sided glass mirror, but there was a camera installed in the corner of the ceiling facing directly at me. After I was instructed where to sit, the female and the male agent sat across from me and opened a floodgate of questions.

The female agent introduced herself to me again. "My name is Special Agent McGee and this is my partner, Special Agent Fletcher." They extended their hands for me to shake, but I refused. When they realized that I wasn't going to shake their hands, they sat down and got straight to why I was here.

Special Agent McGee started off the conversation. "Since you know why you're here, tell us why you murdered Mr. and Mrs. Nichols?"

"I haven't murdered anyone."

"Your prints are in their house."

"They can't be if I wasn't there."

"We also have your fingerprints on the check your sister,

Alayna, tried to deposit in her bank account," Agent McGee pointed out.

Surprised by her assertion, I sat there, trying to think of an explanation for my fingerprints being on the check, and then it came to me. "The reason why my fingerprints are on that check is because Alayna showed it to me. She was so excited about the deal she made with the couple and wanted to show me proof."

"So you're saying that she handed you the check and that's why your fingerprints were on it?"

"Yes, that's exactly what I am saying."

"Well, tell us why your DNA is all over the crime scene?" Agent Fletcher interjected.

"I can't tell you why."

"And why is that?" Agent McGee chimed back in.

"I was hoping that you could tell me."

Agent McGee chuckled. "Agent Fletcher, it looks like we have a comedian on our hands."

"Yes, it definitely seems that way," Agent Fletcher agreed.

"Look, I don't wanna waste you all's time. Take me to jail, because I don't have anything else to say."

"Are you sure you wanna end this interview?" Agent McGee wanted clarity.

"Yes."

"All right, then, I'm gonna have the marshals take you to Tidewater Regional Jail," Agent McGee told me, and then she and the other agent stood up and exited the room.

Not too long after they left me in that cold-ass room, two U.S. Marshals entered and handcuffed my wrists and shackled my ankles. I treaded very carefully to a car that was awaiting my arrival outside of the federal building. Once inside the car, they made sure that I was safe and secured to the backseat's seat belt. Immediately thereafter, they started the engine and proceeded to the nearest ramp to the interstate and headed east in the direction of Tidewater Regional.

"You comfy back there?" one of the marshals asked me.

"Nah, do you wanna take my place?" I asked sarcastically.

"Oh, no . . . I'm fine right where I am."

"I'm sure you are."

I sat in the backseat of this cop car pissed off at myself for being so careless. For the first time, I could admit that I let the money control me. If only I had been able to control my temper. Or at the least, found a better way to kill those people and not leave any evidence that I had been there.

Damn! What was I going to do now?

CHAPTER 24

Alayna

As soon as Alonzo told me that I needed to pick up the money he stashed away in his room, I knew that I couldn't waste any time going over there. I also knew Tim's schedule and knew he wouldn't be there right now, so this would be the perfect time to go there.

When I pulled up in the parking lot of the fire station, I noticed that the main truck was gone, so I knew the firefighters were on an emergency call. What incredible timing for me . . .

Without hesitation, I let myself in the station and walked directly to Alonzo's room. I scanned the room for the air filter box and there it was, only a few feet away from me, near the TV mounted on the wall. I searched Alonzo's room for a screwdriver and couldn't find one, so I went outside to the supply room and grabbed a screwdriver. I returned to Alonzo's room and unscrewed the screws and out came the cash he told me that he had stashed away. I felt like a leprechaun finding gold at the end of the rainbow. I quickly tucked the money inside my front pocket, screwed the screws back into place, and got the hell out of there.

Jesse startled me as I pushed open the exit door to leave. He was coming in from outside. "Oh, wow! You scared me," I said as I placed my right hand over my heart.

"Sorry about that. I thought that was your car parked out there. What brings you by?"

"Had to get something that I left in my room," I lied.

"Tim told me that you quit."

"Yeah, I did. I'm gonna pursue other endeavors." I lied to him once again.

"I feel like you quit because of me and the relationship Tim and I have," he commented. And I believe, with that little smug look he wore on his face when he said it, that he was rubbing my face in the mud.

I sighed heavily, because he was about to make me curse his ass out. "No, it had nothing to do with you and Tim. I'm good. The person you should be having this conversation with is his wife," I replied sarcastically.

"Believe me, I've had my moments."

"So, tell me, how long has this fantasy of yours involving him been going on?"

"Oh, awhile now."

"Does it bother you that he'll never leave his wife for you?"

"Nope. I couldn't care less. I'm just having fun."

"If you call getting caught on your knees sucking on another man's dick fun, then I feel sorry for you."

"Don't feel sorry for me. Feel sorry for your brother. It seems as though he has gotten himself in a little pickle."

"You can call it what you want, but he's going to be fine. I can assure you of that. Oh, and when he gets out, I'm gonna make sure he knows what kind of person he's working around," I threatened, and then I walked off. I couldn't tell you if Jesse stood there or entered the station, because I refused to turn around. I wouldn't give him that satisfaction. Instead, I got in my car and hauled ass out of the parking lot. With Alonzo's money in my pocket, I drove back home so I could put it away. I would hold on to it until Alonzo told me what to do with it.

When I arrived home, I kept my cell phone by my side, just in case Alonzo called me. But after I waited for hours, he didn't call back. I did, however, get a couple of unexpected visitors. You should've seen my face when Levi came into our bedroom telling me that there were two federal agents at my front door. I don't know why, but I instantly became uptight. But then I remembered that they had just arrested my brother earlier in the day, so why not be angry with them?

I climbed off my bed and made my way down the hallway and greeted them at the front door, where Levi left them standing. The front door was slightly ajar, so I grabbed hold of the doorknob and pulled the door toward me just a little more. I wanted to get a full view of these two assholes.

"If it isn't Special Agent McGee and her flunky. How may I help you on this fine night?" I asked in a cynical manner.

"We stopped by to see if we could get a few minutes of your time," she answered.

"Didn't we just have this same conversation back at the bank?"

"Yes, we did. But after arresting your brother a few hours back, we were hoping that you'd come to your senses."

"I didn't have anything to say to you then, and I don't have anything to say to you now," I hissed at her, and then I moved to slam the door in her face, but she blocked it with her foot.

"Not so fast," she said.

I looked down at her foot and then I looked back up at her. "Lady, if you don't move your damn foot, you're gonna find yourself limping around on it for the next couple of weeks," I warned her.

"You know that I'm going to make sure that your brother never gets out of jail."

"Is that a question or what?"

"I know he murdered that couple, and if you don't tell me what happened, I'm gonna put you in a cell next to his and I'm gonna make sure that you never see the light of day."

I chuckled loudly and laughed in her face. "Listen, RoboCop, you have nothing on me, because if you did, I'd be in handcuffs right now. So stop harassing me before I get my attorney on you. You're becoming a nuisance."

"Does your husband know that you tried to cash a thirty-thousand-dollar check from a dead couple? And did you tell him that we put a freeze on your joint bank account?" She wouldn't let up. And what was so damaging was that Levi heard our entire conversation. He was standing a few feet behind me, and I didn't even know he was.

"Alayna, what is she talking about?" he asked as he revealed himself. He stood in clear view of the federal agents.

"We'll talk about that later," I told him, hoping to get rid of him. But it didn't work. He stood there and turned his full attention toward the agents.

"You said that she tried to cash a thirty-thousand-dollar check?" he asked the female agent.

"Yes, as a matter of fact, she did. We froze your bank account too," Agent McGee added. And when she uttered those words, I tried to close the door on her foot again, but Levi made it difficult to do so.

"This is the last time I'm gonna tell you to move your feet!" I threatened her.

Levi grabbed me and pulled me away from the front door. I stumbled a bit, but I managed not to lose my balance.

"What did you do that for?" I roared. I was caught off guard and angry at how Levi had just manhandled me in front of two federal agents. It felt like he had taken their side.

"I'm gonna get to the bottom of this shit," he said, and turned his focus toward the agents.

"You fucking son of a bitch! You're gonna stand there and listen to those people over your wife?" I roared once again. Because how dare he treat me like that in front of these people that were trying to lock me up! They were the fucking enemy. Not me.

"But you're not giving me anything. They're telling me about a fucking check written out to you, and the check owners are dead now, Alayna. So make this make sense to me?" he shouted back at me.

"Fuck you!" I hissed, and then I grabbed my purse and exited my house. I knew I had to get away from this place before I said something that would incriminate myself. And Levi wasn't helping my situation at all. He was acting like he was riding for them. He didn't acknowledge the fact that I had just walked out of the house. He just let me leave and stood there in the doorway and gave Agent McGee and her partner his undivided attention. While Agent McGee spilled the beans on me about the check and who it belonged to, I witnessed Levi let those federal agents into my home and close the door. I didn't know if he was going to let them search the place or what. All I know was that he literally turned his back on me. He definitely showed me another side of him today.

When I walked by him on the way out of the house, I should've shoved him on the fucking floor. He really had proven to me where his loyalty lay, so there was no need for me to stick around.

After I got into my Jeep, I looked back at my apartment once more before I drove away. I shook my head in disappointment, knowing that Levi had chosen their side over mine. Now I needed an ally, but who could that be?

I couldn't think about nowhere else to go but to Pricilla's apartment. I knew she was probably at home watching reality shows, so I wouldn't be interrupting her from doing anything important. Besides that, I knew that she had talked to my brother again and I wanted to know how he was doing.

It only took her four knocks to open the front door. By the look on her face, I knew she was surprised to see me. "What brings you out this late at night?" she asked. I knew it was five minutes after ten, so I didn't bother to look down at my wristwatch.

"You are not going to believe what just happened . . ." I started off saying as I walked across the threshold into the living-room area of her house.

While she was closing the front door, I saw down on the living-room sofa.

"Tell me," she replied as she walked toward me.

"Those same two Feds that arrested Zo earlier came to my fucking house."

"No way."

"Yes, they did. And when I tried to close the front door on the RoboCop bitch, she stuck her foot in the door and prevented me from closing it."

"That bitch is bold."

"That ain't it. She started getting loud and Levi heard her talking and brought his ass to the front door, pushes me out the way, and starts asking her questions. He did a real live WWE on my ass and disregarded the fact that he was supposed to be on my side instead of going against me."

"Did she bring up Zo's name?"

"Of course, she did. Before I left the house, she was telling him that Zo gave me a thirty-thousand-dollar check and that he killed the old couple, and that if I didn't save my own ass, she was going to lock me up in a cell next to him and I won't ever see daylight again."

"And what did Levi say?"

"He was more shocked than anything, because I didn't tell him about the check, nor did I tell him the real reason why our bank account was frozen."

"Whatcha think he's going to do, now that she told him all that?"

"He's not going to do shit but sweat me about going against Alonzo."

"But that's your brother."

"I know. But Levi doesn't care about that. He doesn't really like Zo all that much."

"Why not?"

"Because of that bet they made a while back. You remember them betting on the game?"

Pricilla chuckled. "Wait, he's still upset behind that?"

"Yep."

"He needs to get over it. It's not the end of the world."

"Tell me about it. And speaking of which, have you spoken to him again?"

"Yeah, they have him in a cell block now."

"How is he doing? Mentally?"

"He sounds like he's okay for the moment. His main thing is getting the lawyer down there to see him."

"Did you pay the retainer yet?"

"Yep, I took it to him right before it got dark outside."

"What did he say?"

"He basically said the same thing he did when we saw him at his office. But, wait, he did tell me that he'll be able to visit Zo at the jail after he's done with two of his other cases that he has in court tomorrow."

"I know you can't wait until he comes home," I said.

Before Pricilla could respond, someone knocked on the front door. *KNOCK! KNOCK! KNOCK!* It startled me, because there was no doubt in my mind that that knocking didn't come from those two federal agents.

"Who is it?" Pricilla asked as she stood up from the sofa.

"It's your brother, girl. Open the door!" a man's voice shouted from the other side of the front door.

After hearing Pricilla's brother's voice, I let out a sigh of relief.

As soon as she opened the door, two guys walked in. It was K-Rock and Russell. K-Rock's real name was Keith and he was Pricilla's younger brother; he was twenty-five years old. Russell was his homeboy that he hung out with, and I assumed that he was around the same age as K-Rock. They were known for robbing local drug dealers around the neighborhood and smoking lots of weed. Of course, K-Rock had tried to push up on me a few times, but he knew that I don't fuck around with thugs, especially since I was a volunteer firefighter and paramedic. Dating him wouldn't be good for my image.

"What's up, pretty girl?" K-Rock asked as he walked into the apartment. I swear, he looked just like the late DMX when he was young.

I smiled. "You tell me."

"What's up?" Russell chimed in. He looked more like the boxer Floyd Mayweather.

"Hi, Russell," I responded as they both stood in the middle of the living-room floor.

"What brings y'all by?" Pricilla wanted to know as she sat back down on the sofa next to me.

"Mama told me that the Feds locked up Zo," K-Rock replied.

"Yeah, they picked him up right while we were at our cake-tasting appointment."

"Mama said it was behind killing somebody?" K-Rock continued, and sat down on the couch across from Pricilla and me.

"Yeah, they're trying to say that he killed an old couple and robbed them. But that's straight bullshit!"

"Damn! When Mama first mentioned it, I was like, damn, Zo going hard out here in these streets," K-Rock commented.

Russell chuckled and sat down next to K-Rock. "I said the same thing."

"So, where they got him at?" K-Rock wanted to know.

"He's locked up in Tidewater Regional," Pricilla answered.

"I've got plenty niggas in there, just in case something jumps off, so he's gonna be fine," K-Rock acknowledged. "Got him a lawyer yet?"

"Yeah, I gave Jeff Swartz his retainer tonight, so he's going to see Zo tomorrow after he's through with court.

"Whatcha think about him as Zo's lawyer?" I chimed in, looking straight at K-Rock.

"He's good. He got a nigga I know from uptown off on a gun and a drug charge. And the nigga was guilty as hell."

"Think he's worth a twenty-five-thousand-dollar retainer?" Pricilla asked K-Rock.

"For murder? Definitely."

"Think he could get Zo off?" Pricilla's questions continued.

"Judging from his representation, I think he can," K-Rock agreed. "But do you think he did it?"

"Keith, what kind of question is that? Of course, he didn't!" Pricilla protested.

"Yeah, my brother isn't capable of doing something like that. He loves people. How do you think he does what he does as a firefighter?"

"Just because you're a firefighter doesn't mean that you aren't capable of killing somebody," K-Rock added.

"Yeah, I know a teacher who killed somebody," Russell chimed back in.

"Well, Zo isn't that person. He's a good guy. He'll give you the shirt off his back," Pricilla said out loud.

"Yeah, that's not his MO." I had to agree with Pricilla. My brother was a teddy bear. He was a hustler, and just recently started this insurance scheme, but he was no killer. Not now, not ever. Well, that is, if he wasn't defending himself. I could see him kill in that moment.

"Keep in mind that when you're put in a desperate position, you'll do anything," K-Rock mentioned.

"Look, I don't care how you look at it, Zo wouldn't kill anyone." Pricilla stood her ground.

"What would you do if you found out later that he did kill those people?" K-Rock pressed the issue.

"I wouldn't do anything, because I know that he didn't do it." Pricilla didn't back off.

K-Rock threw up his hands. "A'ight, you win." He saw that he wasn't getting anywhere with his sister, and he left well enough alone. He did tell Pricilla his real reason for coming there. "I know you're going through something right now, but think you could lend me fifty dollars?"

"Whatcha need fifty dollars for?" Pricilla wanted to know.

"I'm trying to get me some loud and a bottle of Henny," K-Rock told her.

I chuckled. "I can't believe that he didn't lie about it."

"I don't do that," he told me.

"I'll let you work for it," Pricilla insisted.

"What do I have to do?" he wanted to know.

"Detail me and Zo's car."

"Yeah, I can do that. That's nothing. But we're gonna have to do it tomorrow," K-Rock announced. "Do you need us to detail your car too?" he asked me.

"No, I'm good. But if I ever need you two to do a job for me, I'll hit you up," I assured them.

"Sounds good to me," K-Rock replied.

Pricilla gave K-Rock the fifty dollars, and not too long after that, he and his friend Russell left the house. I stuck around and managed to fall asleep on Pricilla's couch.

CHAPTER 25

Tim

I SETTLED INTO BED AFTER KIRSTEN COOKED A HUGE DINNER. AFTER making me pick up a can of tomato paste and ground beef, she elected to cook meat loaf instead. I didn't bitch about it, because meat loaf was my favorite, and she made mashed potatoes with brown gravy and cabbage as the side meal. After I had gobbled that down, I took a hot shower and climbed into bed. While I watched television, my cell phone started ringing. When I looked at the caller ID and noticed it was Jesse, I answered, and hoped that he wasn't calling me with bad news.

"Hey, Jess, what can I help you with?"

"I was calling to check in with you," he told me.

"Is there something wrong?"

Jesse chuckled. "No, silly. I just wanted to hear your voice."

"You know this is not a good time for that?"

"Stop being so uptight. Live a little."

"Is that all you called me for?"

"Well, since you mentioned it, Alayna stopped by the station earlier."

"What did she say?"

"She didn't say much. She did defend Alonzo, saying that he didn't kill those people. But, of course, you and I both know that he did."

"Why would you bring that up to her?" I asked.

"It sure sounds like you're taking her side." Jesse became defensive.

"I'm not taking her side. You just shouldn't be discussing it. That's a very sensitive topic."

"But you are the one that told me about it."

"I know. I know. But that conversation was between you and I. Not you and her."

"Well, let's face it, he did it, and he shouldn't ever be let out of prison. He should rot in there."

"Yes, he should. But let's leave that alone for right now. We can talk about it when I get back to work," I cautioned him.

"Are you coming back in tomorrow?"

"Yes, I will be there. So have a good night."

"Could you at least blow me a kiss?"

"No. You know I can't do that right now."

"So I take it your wife is there with you?"

"Jesse, have a good night and I'll see you tomorrow."

Jesse sucked his teeth. "You do the same." And then he ended the call.

"Was that one of the new guys from the station?" Kirsten asked me. I swear, she came from out of nowhere. It was like she was in the bedroom with me the entire time. She damn near scared me. But then again, it didn't surprise me—that was why I knew it would've been a bad idea to blow a kiss at Jesse over the phone. Kirsten was always around, somewhere.

"Yes, that was Jesse."

"How is he working out for you and the other guys at the station?" she asked, and flopped down on the edge of the bed. I watched her as she untied her sneakers and slide them off her feet.

"He's doing okay. Had to reprimand him a few times, but he's cool for the most part," I explained. Truth be told, I didn't really have any problems with Jesse. He held his own while at the station and in the field. But I couldn't let on to Kirsten that my work relationship was great with Jesse. If I made her think that he was mediocre, and that I had to talk to him periodically, it would send the message to her that there was no favoritism there. And if she found out that I was spending more time with him, she'd look at it like he was in need of training. That was it.

"Tell me, whose side he thought you were taking when you two were just on the phone?"

I started to lie, but then I remembered that when my wife asked me a question, she already knew the answer.

"Alayna."

"And why were you taking her side?"

"He said that she stopped by the station and they had a few words concerning Alonzo's arrest. So I told him that he shouldn't have spoken to her about it. It just wasn't his place. And he got bent out of shape because of it."

"Do you feel like you were taking her side?"

"No."

"Well, then, it's settled," she said, and then she got up from the bed. I watched her as she entered the bathroom, where she started running bathwater. I was truly shocked by her nonchalant dialogue with me. Was I seeing things? Or was she just over the "me and Alayna's situation" and wanted to put it to bed? Either way, I was fine with it. I'd do and say anything right now for some peace around here. With everything going on, getting that was like hitting the lottery.

CHAPTER 26

Alonzo

SPENDING THE NIGHT IN JAIL WASN'T AS BAD AS I THOUGHT IT WOULD be. After my mug shot and fingerprints had been taken, they ushered me to change into an orange jumpsuit, and then they put me in a cell with a young dude that looked like he wasn't a day over twenty-four. He was lying on the bottom bunk when I was let in the cell by the CO, but when he saw me, he got up and moved to the top bunk without me saying a word. Talk about respect.

"Need some help with your sheets?" he asked.

"Nah, I'm good, young blood," I told him, because I didn't need any help, especially not with making my bed. When I climbed inside the wool blanket, I was gonna fuck it up anyway.

"My name is Wayne. What's yours?" he asked as he lay on his back facing the ceiling.

"Alonzo."

"Whatcha in here for?"

"Why don't you tell me what you're in here for?"

"Ima car thief. I can steal whatever kind of car you want."

"What kind of car landed you in here?"

"A 2021 Bentley GT. I pretended to be a valet driver at a ritzy restaurant downtown and scooped it right on up."

"How did you get caught?"

"I fucked around and crashed into another car when I was try-ing to get away."

"Anybody get hurt?"

"Nah, I don't think so," the dude answered. "So, why you in here?" he pressed the issue.

"Murder."

"Hey, wait, they had your picture on TV. You're that fire-fighter guy they said killed those two old people."

"So they say."

"Yo, I swear, you don't look like a killer."

"That's what I keep telling them," I said nonchalantly.

"You sure you didn't do it?"

"Yeah, I'm sure."

"Well, whoever did it sure sliced them up good. They said that blood was all over the kitchen. It looked like some *Texas Chain-saw Massacre*–type of shit."

"Who is 'they'?"

"The newspeople."

"Don't believe everything you hear."

"Did you get a bond?"

"Nope. But my family is working on it."

"I don't wanna be a party pooper, but with your charges, it's gonna be hard as hell to get a bond. If they do, it's gonna be in the millions."

"We'll just have to see, won't we?"

"Hey, you sure you didn't kill those people?"

"Listen, young blood, you've already asked me enough ques-tions for the night. Right now, I just wanna get in this bed and rest up. Is that cool with you?"

"Yeah, man, my bad," Wayne said.

After I shut Wayne down from asking me any more questions, I crawled onto my tiny-ass bed and tried to close my eyes for the rest of the night, but for some reason, I couldn't. I couldn't stop thinking about the charges the Feds had against me, and whether or not I was going to be able to get a bond and get out of this damn place. Was Wayne right? Would the court system make it hard for me to get out? And did Agent McGee have enough evidence against me to keep me locked up forever? I supposed I would find that out pretty soon.

The following morning, after devouring a tray of nasty-ass oatmeal, mystery meat, and old toast, someone called out my name.

"Alonzo Riddick, you have a visit," one of the correctional officers shouted from the door of the cell block. I got up from my twin-size bunk and headed toward the cell block door. A white male CO waited for me. He was a big dude. One of those backwoods, corn-fed dudes, with red hair. His stature was around the same as mine, so he didn't intimidate me at all. I think he was more intimidated by me.

"You Alonzo Riddick?" he asked after I approached him.

"Yeah," I told him.

"Let me see your bracelet," he instructed me.

I flashed him the red plastic bracelet I was wearing, with my photo, name, and inmate number on it. When he confirmed my identity, he told me to turn around so he could handcuff me. After I was handcuffed, he escorted me to the attorney and inmate visiting room. A white man awaited my arrival there. So, when I entered the room, he stood up and greeted me. I shook his hand and introduced myself after the CO uncuffed me.

"Have a seat," he started off, so I sat down. "How are they treating you in here?" he asked.

"I haven't had any problems. Got me in a small-ass cell with another guy. Other than that, I'm not in fear of my life."

Jeff Swartz chuckled as he pulled a couple court documents from his briefcase. "I like your sense of humor," he said. "So I pulled your court records and I see that you're being charged with two counts of first-degree murder, wire fraud, robbery in the first degree, and embezzlement."

"And I am innocent of all those charges." I didn't hesitate to tell him this.

Jeff pulled a yellow legal pad from his briefcase and started writing down a few notes. "On the day in question, could you give a tight alibi?"

"Yes, I can."

"So, where were you on that day?"

"I was out investigating other recent residences where our station had just put out fires." I lied, since I went nowhere but to that couple's house. I just hoped that no one came out later and said that they saw me.

"Do you have those addresses?"

"They're at the station."

"Will I be able to get a copy of them?"

"Sure."

"Okay, so you say that you were visiting other residences, would the homeowners be able to validate that claim?"

"Not all. Because some of the homes are burned down."

"What about the neighbors? Think they could vouch for you?"

"I'm sure they can." I lied once again.

"Did you know the couple in this case?"

"Not personally, no."

"I see that there was a thirty-thousand-dollar check written out to your sister, Alayna. I take it that she knows them, because if she didn't, they wouldn't have written her such a large check? Correct?"

"Yes, she was paid to do a job for them."

"Special Agent McGee doesn't believe it."

"Who cares what she believes? I think she has it out for me."

"She may. But let me tell you something, she feels like she has a great case against you, so she's not going to be satisfied until she gets a judge to keep you behind these bars for the rest of your life."

"But I didn't kill those people. I am a firefighter, for God's sake. I live to keep people alive. Not kill them."

"Well, that's what we're gonna have to prove in court."

"Think we got a good chance at winning this?"

"If you're innocent, then you have nothing to worry about. But I need you to answer this one question."

"What's that?"

"Why were your fingerprints on that check?"

"Because my sister handed it to me. She was so excited when she got it and wanted to show it off. So I grabbed it and looked at it."

"I'll tell you what, if we can get a few people to corroborate your whereabouts on that day, and get some good character witnesses, I think you'll have a chance. But don't get too happy, because the Feds always keep tricks up their sleeves."

"Think I can get a bail hearing, because right now, I have no bond."

"I'm working on that as we speak, but don't get your hopes up. Federal judges aren't inclined to give bonds to people with federal indictments. They like to keep you in jail to prevent you from leaving the country."

"But I'm supposed to be getting married in a few weeks."

"Well, you may have to push the date back," Jeff warned me as he started to shove the court documents and legal pad back into his briefcase. "Think your sister would testify on your behalf?" he added.

"If I told her to, she would."

"Good, because we may need her," he said, and then he stood up from the chair. "I'll talk to you in a couple of days. Try to stay out of trouble." He then pressed the button to have the door open.

I watched in dismay as he left me sitting at the table. Boy, would I pay another twenty-five thousand dollars to him to get him to hide me in his briefcase and take me out of here. Wishful thinking.

On my way back to the cell block, I couldn't help but think about the talk I just had with my attorney. He sounded like he knew his shit. And that made me feel good about the possibility of me winning it. So I could say confidently that I might get out of this thing when it was all said and done.

As soon as I got back inside the cell block, I jumped on the first empty phone and called my sister. When Alayna didn't answer the phone, I hung up and called Pricilla. Thankfully, she answered.

"You have a prepaid call from Zo. To accept this call, press five now," the recording said. Once I heard the beep sound, I knew she had accepted my call.

"Hi, baby," she didn't hesitate to say.

"Hi," I said, and let out a long sigh.

"How are you?"

"I'm okay."

"Did you sleep okay? Have you got into any fights?"

I chuckled. "No, I haven't gotten into any fights. I called you because I need you to call Alayna and tell her that I need her to come down here and see me."

"Okay, I can do that. But is there something wrong?"

"No, nothing for you to worry about."

"Don't you wanna see me too?" she said with enthusiasm.

"Sure, baby, you can come. But when I talk to her, I'm gonna need you to leave the room."

"Okay, if you say so," she said with less enthusiasm. I could tell that she didn't like the stipulation I put on her visit with me. But I figured the less she knew about my plans to get out of this jam, the better off she would be.

"How is everything going? Any of our neighbors looking at you funny, now that they know I'm in jail?" I asked.

"Surprisingly, I really haven't seen anyone. Alayna, K-Rock, and his friend Russell stopped by last night. But that's it. Oh, and speaking of which, the reason why your sister stopped by was because those two agents went to her house and told Levi the real reason why their bank account was frozen and about the murder."

"Are you fucking kidding me?"

"No, babe, I'm not."

"What did Levi say?"

"I'm not sure. But I know that they were all ears," she answered.

"This is not good."

"I know."

"Call her and tell her that I need her to come see me ASAP."

"Okay, I will."

"I love you," I told her.

"I love you too."

I slammed the phone down into the hook and stared at it. My first thought was to call Alayna's house and hope that Levi answered the phone so that I could curse his ass out for running his fucking mouth. But I figured doing that wouldn't be a wise thing. I'd definitely make things bad for me if I did that, so I felt it was best to walk away from the phone and wait for Alayna to come and see me. That way, I could ask her all the questions I needed.

CHAPTER 27

Alayna

I WAS AT HOME, MINDING MY BUSINESS, WHEN LEVI CAME IN FROM work. He was on his lunch break. I was in the bedroom, counting money, when I heard him walk into the house. I hurried and put the money away as I heard the front door close. He came looking for me. He even shouted out my name as he made his way to our bedroom.

"Alayna!" he called out.

I ignored him.

As soon as he opened the bedroom door, he questioned me about it. "Why didn't you answer me when I called you?"

"Because I'm not in the mood to talk."

"So you think our problems are just going to disappear?"

"Levi, what do you want?"

"The Feds are saying that your brother killed those people."

"He didn't do it."

"And how do you know?"

"Because I know my brother."

"The Feds have a mountain of evidence stacked against him and they're going to bury him with it. And if you don't cooperate with them, you're going down, right with him."

"He didn't do it."

"So then, who did it?"

"I don't know."

"Alayna, wake up. Our fucking bank account is frozen because you tried to deposit a thirty-thousand-dollar check that belonged to those dead people. Are you fucking stupid or just plain dumb?"

"Fuck you, Levi! Don't you talk to me like that!" I roared as I shot up from the bed.

"If you don't help yourself, you're going down with your brother," he said, and then he stormed out of the room.

"Fuck you! You have no idea what you're talking about. You believe everything you hear someone tell you," I spat as I rushed to the bedroom door and yelled behind him.

"I know that I ain't going to jail with you or your brother. Especially not for murder!" he yelled back.

"He didn't do it!"

"Wake up! I'm going to my parents' house," he yelled once again.

"Carry your ass! I don't care!" I shouted.

"I know you don't care, and see that's the problem. You know what? You're gonna regret treating me the way you do. Wait and see," he threatened as he made his exit.

"Yeah, whatever!" I shot back.

After I watched him leave, I stood there in the doorway of my bedroom and thought about Levi's words. Did they really have evidence against my brother that they could bury him with? I wonder what else the Feds told Levi. Was he holding out on me? Did he know more than he was telling me?

While I mulled over a few things, my cell phone rang; it was Pricilla. It sounded urgent when she told me that she needed me to come and see her right away. I told her that I would be over quickly.

The drive to her house didn't take long—maybe fifteen minutes. And the whole time, I thought the worst. What information did she have for me now?

She saw me when I pulled up, because she waited for me to approach her as I walked toward her front door.

"We need to go and see your brother."

"What happened?" I asked her as I crossed the threshold.

"He just called and told me to tell you that he needed to see you. He even said that when he talks to you, he wants me to leave the room."

"Why?"

"I don't know."

"Well, let's go," I said.

I turned to leave the apartment and Pricilla followed me.

We took her car and I rode shotgun. "Levi and I just had a big argument," I shared.

"About Zo?"

"Of course. He thinks Zo killed those people."

"Did you tell him that he didn't?"

"Of course, I did."

"And what did he say?" she asked.

"He ignored me. Talking about the Feds has a mountain of evidence against Zo, and that if I didn't look out for myself, then I'm going down with him."

"He's a dickhead!"

"Tell me about it," I agreed.

"Have you talked to Tim again?"

"No."

"That's who we need to talk to. Tim can vouch for Zo. He can tell the Feds what type of person my man really is."

"He's not gonna do it."

"Why not?" she asked.

"Because he cares about no one but himself."

"I think you should still try. Call him now," Pricilla insisted.

"All right, hold on," I said, and then I grabbed my cell phone from my handbag. I called Tim's cell phone and he answered on the second ring.

"Hello," he said.

"Hey, how are you?"

"I'm good, and yourself?"

"I really need a big favor from you."

"What is it?"

"I need you to talk to the Feds."

"And tell them what?" he asked.

"Tell them what kind of person Zo really is. They're painting him to be a monster."

"Nothing I could say to them will make Zo look any better."

"Have you tried?"

"Initially, when they first came and talked to me. Other than that, no," he admitted.

"Well, I think that you should call them."

"I'm not calling them, Alayna. Let those people do their jobs. If Zo didn't do it, then it will come out in court."

"Why not prevent that?" Pricilla yelled out loud as she listened to Tim talk on speaker.

"Is that Pricilla?"

"Yes, it is. And you're a piece of shit, Tim. He would do it for you!" she roared.

"I'm gonna end this call right now," he threatened.

"Don't hang up, Tim," I interceded.

But it was too late. He ended the call. Pricilla's words must have hit below the belt.

"You were right. He ain't shit! But I betcha if the shoe was on the other foot, Zo would do it for him," Pricilla insisted.

"Yeah, I know he would."

"You should call him back and tell him about himself."

"It's not worth it. He's not gonna answer. Let's just get down here and see what my brother wants," I instructed, and turned my concerns toward him.

CHAPTER 28

Tim

AFTER GETTING OFF THE PHONE WITH ALAYNA AND PRICILLA, IT got me thinking that this shit was going to hit the fan. Now they didn't come out and say that I should clean up my end, but the urgency in their tone sure lit the spark up in me. There were at least a dozen people left that owed us money from the insurance scam, and I knew that they were seeing the news. But what they thought about this whole thing was what I was most concerned about. So I got in my car and took a drive over to Amy and Mitch's house. They still owed ninety-five hundred dollars to me and Zo, but I wanted them to know that they could keep the money if they didn't blow the whistle on me for doing the operation.

When I pulled up, I saw the wife outside getting groceries from her car. She looked shook when I approached her, like she saw a ghost or something.

"Hi there, wasn't expecting to see you."

I smiled at her. "Need some help," I offered her, and tried to take the bag of groceries out of her hands.

She pulled back from me. "No, I'm fine," she said, and started making her way toward her front door.

"Where is your husband?"

"He's in the house," she told me as she picked up the speed in her step. "Mitch, Tim is out here!" she yelled from the front step of her porch.

Mitch raced toward the front door and opened it. I swear, I had never seen an old person move so fast. After he opened the door, he let his wife inside. She stood at the doorway with Mitch, while I stood on the front porch.

"What brings you by?" he didn't hesitate to ask.

"I was coming by about the money," I replied.

"We don't have any money. That money is gone."

"No, that's not what I came here for. I came here to tell you that you could keep it."

"We didn't need you to come by here and say that. We already knew we could when we saw that that old couple was murdered in their house a few days back."

I chuckled. "So, wait, what does that have to do with me?"

"We know your partner did that. It's all over the news." Mitch didn't hold back. It seemed like with each word he uttered, he was getting bolder. He was even sticking his chest out.

"My partner didn't do that. It's all just a misunderstanding."

"So you're saying that you did it?" He didn't back down.

"No, I didn't. Listen, Mitch, I don't know why you're coming at me like this. I just came by to say your debt is paid. That's it. All that other stuff isn't necessary."

"You better get off my porch before I call the cops on you," he threatened me.

"Trust me, you don't need to call the cops. I'm leaving of my own free will."

"And don't you come back either!"

I turned to leave, and I couldn't believe how angry I was for the way this old man was treating me. It was no surprise to me that these guys had been watching the news. But what was so crazy was that they really thought that I had something to do with that murder. And if they believed it, then the other home-owners that we had arrangements with might think the same way. I saw that this thing was worse than expected. I was gonna have to clear my name now before it blew up in my face. After I stepped down off the porch, I turned around and noticed that Mitch and Amy were still standing at the front door. So I said, "If I find out that you talked to the cops, I'm gonna call the insurance company on you and tell them how you were a willing participant in this whole insurance scam. And you're going to go to jail and probably spend the rest of your natural lives there. So think about that when your hand itches to call the cops on me."

"Close the door, Mitch!" Amy urged her husband. So he did. I looked over my shoulders twice, and both times I noticed that they hadn't left the front door. They wanted to know for sure that I had left their premises.

As I drove away, all I could think about was how Amy and Mitch treated me, and I realized that I was gonna have to think of a master plan. One that was going to get me a "get out of jail free" card. And the only way to do that was to call my friend Bobby back.

I pulled out my cell phone and called his number. He didn't answer, so I left him a voicemail message. But what do you know, because as soon as I left him a message, he called me right back. I pulled over to the side of the road. I knew that I couldn't drive and concentrate on what I was going to tell him.

"Hey, buddy, what's going on?" Bobby asked.

"Remember what I was telling you about a few days ago?"

"Yeah, sure."

"I need you to make that call for me."

"To my detective friends?"

"Yes."

"When would you like to talk to them?" he asked.

"Today. Now, if you can."

"Okay. Let me make some calls and I will call you right back."

"I'll be waiting," I said, and then we ended the call.

After we got off the phone, I drove back onto the road. I headed to the station. Going home wouldn't be a good place to talk to the cops, especially around my wife. It wouldn't end well.

As soon as I pulled into the station, my cell phone rang and it was Bobby. "Hey, did you make the call?" I wanted to know.

"Yep, but they aren't working that case anymore. The Feds took it over. So call Special Agent McGee. I have her number if you need it."

"I've spoken to her before. I have her card."

"Sounds like you're gonna need an attorney present before you sit down with her."

"I haven't done anything wrong, so that won't be necessary," I said.

"Would you like for me to be present when you talk to her?"

"Sure, can you do that?"

"Absolutely. I'm off today. I'll be by there in an hour," Bobby said.

"Great, see you then."

As soon as I got off the phone with Bobby, I pulled out Agent McGee's cell phone number and dialed it.

"Agent McGee," she answered.

I was sitting in my car watching Jesse and Paul while they were cleaning the ambulance and said, "Hi, Agent McGee, this is Chief Tim over at the station, I think we need to talk."

"Sounds like music to my ears," she said. "Wanna come to my office, or shall I come to yours?"

"I would prefer for you to come to mine. But do you think it would be in my best interest to call my attorney?"

"Have you committed any murders?"

"No."

"Then there's no need to have any attorney present."

"When can you be here?" I asked.

"My partner and I can come now."

"Give me an hour."

"Okay, see you then."

Immediately after I ended the call with Agent McGee, I climbed out of my car and made my way into my office. I took out a pen and pad and began to write down every insurance scam Zo and I did and how much money we made from it. I knew the Feds were going to need this information when I finally got a chance to sit down and speak with them about it. It's time to think about my own ass. I had too much to lose and Alonzo wasn't worth losing it over.

I swear, it felt like the clock was moving slowly. One hour seemed like it took an entire day. And when Special Agent McGee and her partner walked into my office, it seemed like they were walking in slow motion. Thankfully, Bobby walked in right after them, because I needed him to be around for moral support.

I extended my hands to everyone that entered my office and told each one where to sit. Special Agent McGee pulled out a tape recorder and placed it on my desk. She indicated that she needed to document everything I was going to say to her. She introduced herself, her partner, and provided my name, time, and date of this recording. Bobby sat there in his civilian clothes and listened intently.

"Tim Stancil, do you give me permission to record this interview?"

"Yes, I do," I said.

"Okay, we're ready," she announced.

"I'm here today to set the record straight about my dealings and what I know about the murders of Mr. David Cole and the couple Arthur and Beatrice Nichols."

"Wait, you know something about David Cole's murder?" Agent McGee interrupted me.

"Yes."

"Okay, continue."

"For the last couple of years, Alonzo Riddick and I have been committing insurance fraud with fire victims. Our role was to write out damage reports to the insurance companies, embellish the extent of the fires so the homeowners could get bigger payouts. If we get the homeowners a one-hundred-thousand-dollar payout, we demand that they give us twenty-five thousand dollars, because the damages only amounted to forty thousand or fifty thousand in reality. So, when the insurance policy is processed, we tell the homeowner to give us a payout of, let's say, nine thousand every week until the debt is paid. It's never a huge amount. It's always dragged out."

"Why only a few thousand a week, not a lump sum?" McGee asked me.

"Because it wouldn't look suspicious at the bank when the homeowner took out that limited kind of money."

"Oh, so they give you and Alonzo cash money?"

"Yes."

"Okay, continue."

"Well, when their debt is paid, we move on to the next home-owner, and it's been going on for the past couple of years."

"Who picks up the money?"

"Sometimes I do it, and sometimes Alonzo does it."

"How much have you made off those insurance fraud cases?"

"Maybe a little over a million dollars."

"Separately?"

"Yes, separately. He made about a million and I got the same amount."

"So, where is this money?"

"It's been spent. When money like that comes through your hands, it goes out as soon as it comes in."

"Do you have any more of this money laying around?"

I wanted to tell her that I had a little bit left, but I knew that she would confiscate it, so I told her that it was spent.

"Tell me about the murders." She moved the conversation along.

"Which one?"

"It's up to you."

"Okay, well, I didn't know that Alonzo had killed the man from Lake Edward until I saw it on the news."

"So you weren't there?"

"No."

"Then how do you know that he killed him?"

"Because I knew that he had just left his house to get the money that he owed us. And when I saw it on the news that the man was dead, I knew that Alonzo did it."

"Did you question him about it?"

"Yeah, I did. I went to his room and asked him if he killed

Mr. Cole when he picked up the money, and he denied it. But I know Alonzo, lately he's been coming loose at the seams since he's been planning his wedding. He's been jumpy and he's been intolerable lately. He's turned into a different guy. Not this cool, calm, and gentle giant everyone had grown to love."

"So, when you questioned him about the murder, he said that he didn't do it?"

"Yeah, he said that he didn't do it, but I know he did. He had just left the man's house from making a pickup."

"Tell us about the Nichols couple. What do you know about that? And were you there?"

"No, I wasn't there either. But I know he did it."

"Did you ask him about it?"

"Of course, I did."

"Did he deny doing that too?"

"Yeah, he did. But once again, those people owed us a lot of money, and the only reason Alonzo would kill them was if they didn't want to pay up."

"So you have no evidence about him committing those murders? But you have a hunch?"

"Yeah, I know he did it."

Agent McGee leaned forward and stopped the recording. Then she sat back in her seat. "I need evidence, Tim, not a hunch." She let out a long sigh.

"So you can't tie him to the murders with the insurance scams alone?"

"Yeah, we can, but that's not enough. I need physical evidence. A freaking confession."

"I can get him to confess."

"And how do you propose to do that?"

"I could ask him again."

"Did he confess to you the first time you asked him?"

"No."

"Then what makes you think he's going to do it now? He's incarcerated. And there's absolutely no way he's going to confess to a murder over those jail-recorded phone calls. I need more,"

Agent McGee said, and then her cell phone rang. "Give me a minute." She stood up from her chair. She exited my office and walked out to the hallway. I tried to listen in on her call, but she wouldn't utter a word. All she acknowledged to the caller was that she was listening to them.

I turned my attention toward Bobby, and I could see the shame on his face. He looked like he wanted to distance himself away from me. Boy, did he make me feel small sitting behind my desk.

A few minutes later, Agent McGee reappeared. "Got a witness that can put Alonzo at the scene of David Cole's residence at the time of the murder," she said joyfully.

I hit my desk with my fist. "I told you he did it."

"Now all we need is another witness. Someone that could put him at the Nichols place on the day they were murdered."

"You will. Don't worry. Just put it on the news or something. Let the public know that you need their help," I told them with eagerness. From the outside looking in, I looked like I was cheering on the cops by making sure they collected as much evidence as they could so that they could lock Alonzo up forever. He needed to be taken off the streets for good because he was a very dangerous man.

Agent McGee grabbed the recording from my desk. "You make sure you don't leave town."

It was like I hadn't just given her a ton of fucking information that she could use for her murder case. What an ungrateful bitch.

"Where would I go?" I asked her sarcastically. But I was more shocked at her candor than at anything else.

"Come on, partner, let's go," she said, and then she exited my office.

The moment she left, Bobby stood up and made the same declaration. "Let me get out of here. Gotta get ready for work."

"But I thought you said that you were off today?" I asked him. I mean, just over an hour ago, this asshole told me that he would come by my office and support me, because he didn't have to go to work today, and now all of a sudden, he had to go. What a lying motherfucker!

I started to call him out on it, but then I decided against it. He had already shown me his cards. As soon as he left my office, I would never hear from him again, and that was cool. I saw I was gonna have to fight this thing on my own. The good thing was, I was not implicated in the murders. I could turn witness for the Feds and get them to give me immunity on the insurance scam side of it. I knew I was gonna lose my job now, since I'd blown the whistle. But I'd rather bag up groceries in a store than sit behind bars.

That was my story and I was sticking to it.

CHAPTER 29

Alonzo

WHEN MY SISTER AND PRICILLA SHOWED UP FOR MY VISIT, I WAS happy as hell. Like planned, I spoke with my fiancée and then sent her off on her way so that I could have Alayna alone. Pricilla didn't seem too happy that she had to leave so soon. But my life was on the line and I had to think about myself.

"Pricilla told me about the Feds showing up to your crib."

"Yeah, they filled Levi's head up with a lot of bullshit and left me to pick up the pieces."

"I'm gonna need you to go to the station and fill out a couple of fire reports with my locations being anywhere other than at David Cole's and that old couple's house."

"Sure, I can do that. But what addresses do you want me to use?"

I thought for a second. "I'll tell you what, rewrite them and put Tim's name on all of them. Make it look like I didn't go to any of their houses. Think you can handle that?"

"Of course," she said, and then she gave me a serious look. "What if he finds out that I changed the reports?"

"Fuck him! And besides, he's gonna have to prove that you did it." I instantly became irritated by the fact that she cared about what Tim would say when he found the new reports. And then Alayna's facial expression changed. "What's wrong?" I asked her.

"Did you do it?" She came out of nowhere and asked me that!

"No, of course not." But I knew that she wasn't buying my lie. Alayna was my sister. We grew up in the same house. She knew when I was lying to her.

"Come on, big bro! You know I got you either way. But I gotta know what I'm getting myself into."

I looked down at the table I was sitting at and then I looked back up at her. It took a lot out of me, but I knew I needed to tell her the truth. I nodded my head.

She let out a long sigh. "It's okay. We're gonna get through this."

And, I swear, hearing those words was like music to my ears. I knew she was going to have my back no matter what, and I wanted to tell her the truth, but I couldn't will myself to do it. I just didn't want to see the disappointment in her face. I knew she would see me as a monster if she really knew the truth, so I felt the need to keep the lie going. Keep her in the dark just a little bit more.

"So you're gonna handle that for me?" I needed reassurance.

"Yeah, I gotcha."

"Please don't tell Pricilla. She won't take it as well as you."

"Don't worry about her. I got her."

"So, when are you going to do it?"

"As soon as I leave here."

"You can't let Tim catch you doing it."

"I won't. And speaking of which, I talked to him right before I got here."

"He called you?"

"No, I called him."

"What did he say?"

"I asked him to call the Feds and speak up for you, but in so many words, he told me no. He wasn't getting in it."

"I knew he was going to turn on me. Fucking piece of shit! It's just me and you now, sis."

"And I've got your back all the way until the wheels fall off."

I placed my hands on the glass partition that divided me and Alayna. "You know I love you for this, right?"

She placed her hand in the same spot on the other side of the glass. "Never question my loyalty for you. All right?"

"All right," I said to her. We both removed our hands. "If Levi gives you any more problems, you know that you're more than welcome to stay with Pricilla."

"I know. But he's gonna stay at his mama's house. He told me this afternoon before I came here."

"Fuck him! He's a pussy anyway."

"I wished I would've listened to you before I tied the knot with that loser."

"You still got time to divorce him," I said, and started chuckling.

"After we get you out of jail, that's the first thing on my to-do list."

"And I'm gonna pay for it." I continued to laugh and then I turned my focus to four people coming in my direction. It was two COs and Agent McGee and Agent Fletcher. She was the only one smiling as she approached me. Both COs grabbed me, and Agent McGee pulled out her handcuffs and slapped them on my wrists. On the opposite side of the glass partition, Alayna stood up and started screaming obscenities. "Alonzo Riddick, you are under arrest for the murder of David Cole," Agent McGee announced.

I started chuckling, because this woman was tripping and I wasn't going to give her the satisfaction in letting her see me sweat.

"He's already in jail. Why the fuck she's arresting you all over again?" Alayna screamed through the partition.

A few seconds later, Pricilla dashed back into the visiting room. "What's going on?" she shouted.

"I don't know. I can't hear what she's saying, but he's being arrested," I heard Alayna say.

Agent McGee didn't acknowledge what Alayna or Pricilla was doing on the other side of the glass. I could tell that she was relishing in the thought that she was arresting me for killing Mr. Cole. I remained silent while all four officers carried me away from the visiting room. All eyes were on me as I was led out of there.

"Call my lawyer," I managed to yell out to Alayna. I didn't believe she heard me though.

While McGee and Fletcher placed me inside the unmarked car, I saw her smile at me. In my eyes, it was more of a smirk. But, nevertheless, I asked her about it.

"You find humor in this?"

"I just can't wait to see the look on your face when a federal judge hands down a life sentence to you."

"But I didn't do anything wrong. I didn't kill anyone," I said calmly.

"Tell that to the judge."

"You love locking our people up, huh?"

"Mr. Riddick, don't use that race card with me. I lock people up that commit crimes. And I prove in court that they committed the crime at hand. So spare me with your antics."

"If you say so."

"Correction. I know so," she said, and then she slammed the car door in my face.

Agent Fletcher got behind the driver's side and drove us away from the jail. I noticed that he never had much to say during all of our encounters. He pretty much let her run the show and I made mention of it.

"Who wears the pants? You or her?" I asked him.

"We both wear the pants," he replied.

"Bullshit! She runs all over the top of you. I can see that you have no balls whatsoever."

"And you're entitled to your opinion," he answered.

"I bet you let her run the show because you're fucking her."

"Now you're out of bounds," he commented.

"I didn't know that there were boundaries, you pussy!" I insulted him. I honestly wanted to headbutt the nigga and give him an instant headache.

"Just worry about yourself."

"Oh, don't worry, I am." And then I smiled at him. I wanted to let on that nothing he was doing to me was truly affecting me.

"Don't talk to him. He's a lost cause. Getting his ass off the streets is the best thing we can do to protect our community," Agent McGee chimed in.

"See, there she goes, telling you what to do," I pointed out. I wanted to get underneath these agents' skin. They say that misery loves company, and whoever made that up was right. I hated the fact that these two agents had me by the balls. And to add another murder to my jacket was going to be hard to get out of, especially after my lawyer will come back and tell my sister and my fiancée that he's going to charge extra for this new case. There was no way I was gonna get a bail now. I knew that would be out of the question. Pricilla was not going to be happy about this and I might have to switch gears. Figure out a way to implicate Tim into these murders. Shit! It would boil down to his words against mines. I mean, it wouldn't be that far-fetched, since we did this insurance fraud scheme together. It could work if I worked it the right way.

CHAPTER 30

Alayna

PRICILLA COULDN'T HOLD IT TOGETHER AS WE WITNESSED ALONZO being escorted away in handcuffs. She cried out and almost lost her balance, nearly falling to the floor. "Why are they doing this to him?" she shouted.

A CO from our side of the glass approached us and told us that we had to leave. I grabbed Pricilla's hand and led her out of the visiting room.

"We've gotta call his lawyer!" she cried out.

I pulled out my cell phone as soon as we exited the building. When I called Alonzo's attorney's office, his receptionist told me that he wasn't in. So I left him a message and told her that I'd wait for his call.

I saw that Pricilla wasn't in the mood to drive back to her house, so I got behind the wheel and drove. I tried to console her, but I couldn't help her. Instead, I got her mother on the line and had her meet me at Pricilla's apartment. Thankfully, Pricilla's mother was there when I pulled up and I handed her off to her. I got into my car and headed to the station. I knew that if I was going to help my brother, now would be the time to do it, because those agents were on his ass, and they weren't letting up. I could tell that the female agent truly had it out for my brother. It was like she had a personal vendetta against him.

Like they used to fuck once upon a time, long ago, and he broke her heart. I mean, she was going in on him and making sure that she buried his ass. It was sickening to watch. I just couldn't wait until this was all over.

In like a flash of lightning, it seemed like I blew through every red light to get to the fire station to get this deed done for my brother. When I entered the parking lot, I noticed that Tim's car was there, but I knew that I couldn't let that stop me. I was good at avoiding Tim, so now wouldn't be any different.

I tried to sneak into the station from the side door, but I fucked around and ran into Jesse's dick-sucking ass. He was all smiles when we approached each other.

His first words were: "Heard what happened?"

"No, but I'm sure you're gonna tell me."

"The Feds got a witness that puts your brother at the scene of David Cole's murder the night he was killed."

I stopped in my tracks. Now I knew why Zo was being arrested all over again. And if Jesse knew about it, then so did Tim. I refused to utter another word to Jesse and turned to go to Alonzo's office. Jesse saw the swiftness in my steps and inquired about my being there.

"I thought you didn't work here anymore."

"What I do is none of your business," I said without looking over my shoulders. Jesse knew I had to be going to Alonzo's office and made mention of that too.

"Your old office is on the other side of the station. Why are you over here?"

"I've worked here longer than you have and I've been coming to this place since I was a kid, so don't ever question me about what parts of the station I enter. This is, and will always be, my second home, so the quicker you get that through your head, the better off you'll be, okay?"

"My bad little lady! I was just talking shit." He chuckled. I could tell that I caught him off guard with my abrasiveness.

I refused to entertain him anymore and continued on my journey. Alonzo's office was only a few more steps away, so when I arrived at his door, I opened it, went inside, and locked it behind me. I raced over to his desk and pulled out his damage re-ports' pad. And one by one, I started making up fake ones. I made seven of them in all and put Tim's name on it instead of Zo's. I even went into the system and changed the names as well. The ones that were already filed in Zo's desk drawer, I took them and stuffed them down into my purse.

"Yeah, you fucking bastard. Let's see who gets the last laugh. I would prefer to see that asshole in jail than my brother. Besides, he likes men anyway, so he'll fit right in," I mumbled to myself.

While I gloated in my scheme, I heard someone rattle the doorknob. And when they couldn't get it to open, they knocked on the door.

"Alayna, what are you doing in there? Open the door," Tim said.

I tried to ignore him, but it didn't work.

"Alayna, Jesse already told me that you were here."

"What do you want?" I finally asked him, my hands starting to perspire by my misdeeds.

"Open the door!" he ordered me.

So I got up from the chair and opened the door. "What do you want?" I repeated the question, all while giving him attitude.

"What are you doing in here?" he asked as he looked over my shoulders. I could tell that he was trying to see if anything was out of place in here.

"I was looking for some pictures, why?"

"No, you weren't."

"Yes, I was."

"What pictures?"

"The ones we took at the barbecue a couple months back."

"Did you find them?"

"No."

He eased his way by me, and I turned around and watched him.

"Tell me what you were really doing in here." He wouldn't let up.

"I told you already."

"You know they found a witness that says that Alonzo mur-dered Mr. Cole?"

"I don't believe it," I said.

"Well, it's true, and he's going to be locked up for a very long time."

"They have to prove it."

"Oh, they will," Tim stressed.

"And how do you know this?"

"Because the federal agents came by and told me."

"Don't believe everything they tell you. You know that they're gonna implicate you too. Remember, you can go to jail too. You did commit insurance fraud on multiple occasions."

"And you're guilty by association."

"Is that how we're carrying it?"

"It's every man for himself," he said proudly.

"You know what? I wonder what your wife will say if she knew that you played for the other team too?"

"You wouldn't dare."

"You said, 'Every man for himself.'"

"Try it, you little bitch!"

"Oh, so now I'm a bitch?"

"I will ruin you."

"Not before I ruin you," I threatened him, and then I turned back around and started walking toward the exit door of the station.

I heard Tim's footsteps behind me and it alarmed me. I'd never seen this side of Tim. I was not sure of what he was capable of doing in a situation like this. I could ruin his career and marriage. I didn't do any of the insurance schemes, but I accepted the money from it though.

I swear, I couldn't get out of the fire station quick enough. When I got back into my Jeep, I looked over my shoulders and saw that Tim was standing next to the exit door, watching my every move. It kind of spooked me. But as I slowly drove away, the feelings started wearing off.

Once on the road, I got on the phone and called Pricilla. She didn't answer the phone, but her mother did. And when she realized that it was me on the phone, she handed it to Pricilla. "The Feds were there arresting Zo because they think that he killed that man that lives in Lake Edward," I started off saying.

"How do you know that?" she asked between sobs.

"Because I just left the station. Tim told me."

"That's a lie. Zo would never do anything like that."

"I know. And we're gonna prove it in court," I told her. She didn't know it, but I had evidence to get Alonzo out of jail and put Tim's butt in there as a replacement. The paperwork was right in my pocket. Signed, sealed, and ready to go.

"Where are you now?"

"I'm on my way to go and see Zo's attorney."

"Come get me. I wanna go."

"No, I'm gonna need to do this alone," I assured her.

"Are you sure?"

"Yes, I'm sure."

"Okay, well, call me if you need me," she said.

"I will," I agreed, and then I ended the call.

CHAPTER 31

Alonzo

"Y'ALL ARE ARRESTING THE WRONG MAN. I DIDN'T KILL THAT man." I tried to plead my case to the federal agents as they lifted me up from the back of the undercover car.

"That's not what one of the neighbors said," Agent McGee gloated as she rearranged my handcuffs. She tightened them instead of loosening them.

"I don't care what the neighbor said. I know I wasn't there."

"Let's see what the judge says when you have your day in court."

"And when I win, I'm going to need you to give me a public apology," I told her.

"You and I both know that that won't ever happen."

"Me winning the case? Or you not apologizing to me?" I taunted.

"Both."

I chuckled. "Don't make me make you eat those words."

"Is that a threat? You know you're good for that."

"Nope. Not at all."

"And here I thought that you only murdered the old couple. You get around, sir."

"I didn't kill them either."

"You can say that you didn't do it until your face comes off.

You and I both know that you had a hand in those people's murders and I'm going to prove it," she said, and then she fell silent. "Even Tim believes you did it."

"Who? My partner?" I asked her.

"Not anymore. He's going to save himself," she added as they escorted me inside the building. "I know about the insurance fraud. Yeah, he laid everything out. All the money you guys made off the backs of homeowners in exchange for big payouts of insurance checks."

I laughed. But it was a nervous kind of laugh. And as badly as I wanted to tell her to shut the fuck up, I baited her into telling me more.

"I don't know what you're talking about," I replied in pure denial.

"Oh, you know. I've got a huge confession on tape. Telling me and my partner about the millions of dollars you two made fudging fire incident reports, and making the homeowners give you thousands of dollars at given times. Shame on you."

I chuckled again. "Did he tell you that he was the ringleader?" I changed my tune. I couldn't let her talk. It felt like she was getting the best of me and I needed to be heard.

"No, he told me that the whole scam was your idea and that you two been doing it for a couple of years now."

"That's bullshit! It was his idea. He started this whole thing!" I shouted.

But, in reality, my father birthed the whole insurance fraud scheme a long time ago when money started getting tight for the family. He started off doing it alone, but then, when it got too big for him, he brought Tim on board and then I was brought into the fold right after that. But I would never tell this bitch that. I would never let anyone tarnish my father's legacy.

"Whatcha getting upset for? The way he laid down everything, he has your name written all over it as the ringleader."

"I don't care what you say. He started this whole thing. And he's trying to cover his own ass because he's the one that killed those people. Not me." It spewed from my lips. It felt like venom coming from my mouth. I knew I wasn't supposed to say anything, but I couldn't hold it back. Tim was trying to save his own ass. And now it was time for me to bury him.

"So you're saying that Tim committed the murders?" she wanted to know.

"Yeah, he did it." I continued to lie, but the cat was out the bag and there was no turning back for me.

"Which ones?"

"Both."

"You have proof?"

"Yeah, I have proof."

"And what proof do you have?"

"He told me."

"What did he tell you?" she asked as we walked down a long hallway.

"He told me that on the night he went out to pick up the money from the old man, he wasn't trying to pay up and so Tim killed him."

"And when did he tell you that?"

"The night it happened. When he came back to the station."

"How did he say he killed him?"

"He said that he hit him in the throat and the man fell down on the ground. He dragged him in the house, took all the money he had in his safe, and then Tim left."

"If you knew all of this, then why tell me now?"

"Because I thought that there was honor among brotherhood, but now I see that went out the window when he opened his mouth."

"You're willing to say this on record?"

"Yup."

"What about the couple? Mr. And Mrs. Nichols?"

"What about them?"

"Did he kill them too?"

"Yup, he sure did."

"How do you know?"

"Because he told me."

"Well, he's saying that you did it."

"He's lying."

"How did he tell you that it happened?"

"On the morning that it happened, he told me that he was going to make a pickup. I said okay and that I'd see him when he got back. But when he came back, which was a couple hours later, I noticed that he was dressed in a different uniform. I didn't say anything to him about it then. But later that day, when it came on the news that those people were murdered, I asked him about it. He tried to deny it, but I told him that I wouldn't rat him out. He was my bro. So he managed to get up the courage to admit to doing it. And I told him that his secret was safe with me."

"So, in other words, you're condoning murder?"

"No, I'm not. I'm saying that I had my partner's back no matter what," I corrected her.

"To me, that sounds like you're condoning murder."

"Agent McGee, where I come from, your word is all you have."

"So, why the sudden change now?"

"Because he's trying to save his own ass."

"Well, when we get you in this interview room, just be ready to be up front and transparent."

"I will. Don't you worry," I assured her.

The moment we entered the cold room, Agent McGee watched as Agent Fletcher handcuffed me to an iron table. After they felt like I was secure, they sat down across from me and gave me the floor to talk. She made sure she turned on the recorder first. And from that point, her eyes were glued to my mouth. She soaked up every detail I had for her. She interrupted me a few times for clarity. But for the most part, she let me do the talking.

"On the record, can you tell me how much money you and Tim Stancil made during your insurance fraud scheme?" she wanted to know.

"Off the top of my head, I would say a million dollars each."

"Do you have any of that money left?"

"No, I don't." I deliberately lied to her. What did she think I was? Stupid? I wasn't going to tell her about the money I had left in my possession.

"So you're telling me out of a million dollars, you don't have one red cent left?"

"Nope. I wish I did. But I don't. I'm supposed to get married in a few weeks. My fiancée has spent every dime we had. She's supposed to ask her mother for a loan."

"That's hard to believe."

"It may be hard. But it's true. She'll tell you."

"Well, then, tell me how did your sister, Alayna Curry, end up with that thirty-thousand-dollar check?" she asked.

And, I swear, I didn't see that question coming. She came out of thin air with that shit. But I couldn't implicate my sister in this murder. She was off limits.

"When it comes to saying anything about my sister, I stop there," I said flatly.

"But she was caught with the check in her possession, Mr. Riddick. And that check in question belonged to the Nicholses. The couple that was slain in their home."

"But my sister didn't kill them."

"I know. You said that Tim Stancil did the murder. So I need to know, how did Alayna get the check in her hand, and why was her name on it?"

"Because Tim told them to put her name on the check," I finally said. They had my back against the wall.

"Why would Tim get that couple to write the check out to your sister?"

"Because they were having an affair."

Shocked by my admission, Agent McGee said, "They were what?"

"They were sleeping with each other and Tim trusted her."

"Does she know that Tim murdered the Nicholses?"

"No, she doesn't."

"Now how do you expect for me to believe that?" she continued.

"Because if she knew, she wouldn't have taken the check."

"And how do you know that for sure? That kind of money can make people do some awful things."

"My sister is a good girl. She doesn't have an evil bone in her body."

"She may not have 'an evil bone in her body,' but I'm sure she saw the murder on the news."

"Look, she asked me about it and I lied to her and told her that Tim wasn't involved, and that it was some random home invasion or something."

"So she had no time to question Tim about the murder?"

"If she did, she didn't mention it to me."

"I find that hard to believe," Agent McGee stated.

"What's so hard to believe?"

"That he gave her a check written out for thirty thousand dollars and she didn't question him about his involvement in their murder."

"I guess that's just how they do things."

"When we confronted her about the check at the bank, she told us that the check was written out to her because of an interior consultation fee."

"That's what Tim told her to say."

"So that means that she lied to us."

"I wouldn't call it lying."

"Then what do you call it?"

"She was trying to protect her man, I guess."

"Does her husband, Levi, know about this affair?"

"Yes, he found out about it a couple days ago. That's why she quit the station."

"So it wouldn't surprise him if we brought that to his attention?"

"Nope."

"How much do you love your sister?"

"A lot, why?"

"Because we're gonna have to bring her in and question her. And if she says anything different, then we're gonna scrap everything you said here today."

"She'll vouch for me."

"Let's hope so."

"So, what kind of deal are you going to cut me?"

"I didn't know that we discussed giving you a deal. Partner, did we discuss giving Mr. Riddick a deal?" Agent McGee looked at Agent Fletcher.

"Not to my knowledge."

"But I gave you information about two murders."

"You mean three murders."

"Okay, then three. So, what can I get for that?"

"If everything checks out, you'll just go to jail for insurance fraud."

"I'm still gonna get time?"

"Of course, you are. You just can't break the law and think you can get away with it."

"That's bullshit, and you know it," I said, and then I smashed the table with my fist. It seemed like everything I said was in vain.

"Are you still charging me with the murder?"

"Of course, I am."

"So, then, what was all that for? You think I was talking for nothing?"

"I call it doing your civic duty. But in my line of work, when the bad guy gets caught, we make sure they do the time."

"Yeah, whatever," I said, and let out a long sigh.

Immediately after the interview was over, McGee and Fletcher escorted me out of the room and put me in an iron-barred cell and left me sitting in there. I watched both agents as they walked away and I knew that I had fucked up royally. And at any moment, my sister Alayna was going to be drug through the mud and possibly implicated in this murder. I needed to get word to her, but how? I knew that I needed to get her on the phone but whose phone would I use? The agents weren't going to let me call her and give her a heads-up that they were coming for her. So I was fucked.

But then it came to me when I saw a janitor mopping right

outside in the hallway of the glass interrogation room that the
agents had me in. The young Hispanic guy looked at me a few
times as he mopped the hallway floor outside my cell.

"Keep your head up, brother," he said.

And as soon as he closed his mouth, I knew that he was on my
side.

"Wanna make some money?" I asked him in a whisper. "Don't
stop mopping. Just hear me out."

He did as I instructed and kept mopping.

"If you can get word to my sister, she will pay you one thousand dollars."

The Hispanic guy lifted his head and looked at me.

"No, don't look at me. Just tell my sister that they are coming
for her. Let her know that they know that Tim ratted us out."

"Okay, but how would I get the money?"

"Call her and tell her that I said thanks for going to my office,
and to give you one thousand dollars. If you say it like that, she'll
know that you talked to me for real."

"What's her number?" the guy said, showing real interest.

"555-2982."

"What's her name? And what's your name?"

"She's Alayna. I'm Alonzo. Tell her where you saw me and
that Tim has to go. He needs to leave the building ASAP. And
tell her that I said thanks for going to my office and to give you
one thousand dollars. You got it?" I communicated with him, as
best I could, while at the same time looking in the direction of
the agents. I had to make sure that they weren't looking my way.

"Okay, but one thousand dollars, right?" he pressed me.

"Yes, one thousand dollars. And since you know our names,
who are you?"

"Juan. But, wait, I don't think she's going to believe me, my
friend."

I thought for a moment and realized that he might be right. A
strange man calling her and telling her that Tim has to go, and
right afterward asking for one thousand dollars, did seem a bit
suspect. I mean, he could be setting her up, for all she knew. So,

in order for her to believe him, he needed to tell her something that only she and I knew. A childhood secret of some sort.

"Give me some kind of code word," he insisted.

A lightbulb turned on in my head and then it came to me. "Tell her that Alonzo said to remember when we were kids, how I beat up that little girl for taking her ice-cream money after school. She'll definitely believe whatever you tell her after that."

"Okay, no problem. I will tell her."

"Don't forget the other stuff I told you."

"I won't, my friend."

"Thank you."

"No, thank you."

I swear, after giving him that message, it felt like a load was lifted off my shoulders. I just hoped that this guy was going to keep up his end of the bargain and get word to Alayna. I also hoped that he'd remember everything I told him to say. This guy was a wild card, but I figured what did I have to lose? Juan was my only "get out of jail free" card and I intended to try my luck. I mean, what's the worst that could happen? Juan turns out to be an undercover cop, posing as a janitor? Well, in that case, I'd be fucked! But there was only one way to find out.

CHAPTER 32

Tim

I WAS IN MY OFFICE WHEN THE NEWS REPORT FLASHED ABOUT AGENT McGee and her partner making arrests in David Cole's murder. I sat there and watched as she stood in front of the federal building, with David Cole's daughter standing next to her, and addressed a dozen news reporters.

"I called this news conference because I am happy to announce that we have made an arrest in the murder of David Cole. I am standing here with his daughter and other members of his family as a united front that we will bring this murderer, and/or other murderers, to justice for this horrendous crime. Mr. Cole didn't deserve to die in this fashion. He was a great man, and his family and friends loved him. I wanna thank the witness for coming forth with the information that led to the arrest, and to let others know that if you know anything, please come forward. We are also looking for the killers behind the Nichols murders, so, if you have any information there, it would be greatly appreciated. We have to send out a message to these monsters that they cannot just go around and kill at will. These people have loved ones and they deserve to be here on this earth, just like them. So, again, if you have any information, please contact me or my agency. We could keep your name or whereabouts anonymous. We have to stick together, you guys.

And now I'm gonna turn this mic over to his daughter, Sabrina Cole."

I watched as Agent McGee and the daughter of the fallen victim traded places.

She adjusted the mic and then said, "To piggyback off what Agent McGee just said, I want to thank the witness for coming forward, because my father's murderer needs to be brought to justice. My father didn't deserve to be killed. And especially in his own house. That's a major violation. Not only that, and then you rob him of his money. I swear, I hope you rot in jail for what you did to me and my family. You took away a good man. He would give you the shirt off his back. And now he's gone. Gone too soon, I might add. And if it takes every breath out of my body, I'm gonna make sure that you get what's coming to you. You better be glad that I didn't catch you before these federal agents did, because I would be in jail too. You killer!" she roared, and then she looked down around her and stepped away from the podium.

Agent McGee made some more remarks and then she stepped down from the podium. The news conference ended a few minutes later.

After hearing everything that was said, I got up from my desk and decided to go into the TV room, where all the other firefighters congregated when watching TV. It almost felt like they were waiting for me to come into the room, because as soon as I turned the corner, everyone looked in my direction. It was Jesse, Paul, and two volunteers.

Jesse started talking first. "You just watched the news conference?"

"Yeah, I did."

"Is it true?" Paul wanted to know.

"Is what true?"

"Did Zo really kill that man?"

"That's where the evidence is pointing."

"Damn, that's fucked up," one of the volunteers murmured as he scratched his head. He seemed a little perplexed.

"Yeah, that's messed up," the other one agreed.

"So, what's going to happen now?" Jesse asked me.

"I don't know. We'll just have to sit back and see."

"I just can't picture Alonzo killing someone. He's just not that kind of guy," Paul said.

"Neither can I," one of the volunteers said.

"Well, he did. And we're gonna have to deal with the backlash, because it's coming," I warned everyone.

"Think homeowners are going to be afraid to let us in their houses?" Jesse asked me.

"I hope not."

"I know I would be," Paul chimed in.

"Yeah, me too," one of the volunteers mentioned.

"Well, we'll cross that bridge if that happens," I assured them.

"I think we're gonna have to do some damage control. Get in front of this thing. Let the community know that we don't condone that kind of behavior. Let them know that we're on their side and we're going to be transparent with them and that they could trust us," Paul added.

"Yeah, he's right, Captain," one of the volunteers agreed.

"Yeah, you may be right. I'm gonna call my boss and see what we can do."

"Think Alayna knew about it?" Paul wanted to know.

"I'm not sure," I said, because I really didn't know. I mean, those two were close, but for the most part, Alonzo tried to keep a lot of things from her. It was his way of protecting her. So, in this case, it was a toss-up.

"She didn't act like she knew when I saw her earlier," Jesse mentioned.

"She stopped by?" Paul asked.

"Yes, I caught her in Alonzo's office," I said.

"Oh, yeah, she knows something. And you may want to give the investigators a call about it too," Paul agreed.

"And say what?" I wanted to know. I was surprised that he wanted me to rat Alayna out. If he knew how I felt about that, those words probably wouldn't have come out of his mouth.

"Say that you caught her in Alonzo's office. She may have her hands on some evidence that could put him away." Paul made his concerns known.

"Yes, he's right," Jesse chimed back in.

"Well, I'll mention it to them. But that's the extent of it," I told them, saying it with finality.

Jesse noticed the conviction in my voice and gave me a look of disappointment. He knew that I wasn't going to push the envelope with Alayna, and that I was going to protect her as much as I could.

"I think you should prevent Alayna from coming here, moving forward," Jesse suggested. He knew what he was doing by saying that. He wanted to get the reaction from the others. He had an audience, and he was going to take advantage of it to get the feedback he needed.

"Yeah, that would be a good idea," Paul remarked.

"Now I would definitely do that. As a matter of fact, I'm gonna call and tell her."

"She's not gonna like that," Jesse pointed out.

"Who cares what she likes?" Paul blurted out.

"Just settle down, you guys. I'm gonna take care of things from here. Now, if we have any emergency calls tonight, let's deal with them accordingly. Deal?" I ended the conversation, because in my mind, things were going too far. I wasn't implicating Alayna in this situation more than she already was—and that was the bottom line.

"Deal," everyone said in unison.

CHAPTER 33

Alayna

WHEN I ARRIVED AT THE ATTORNEY'S OFFICE, HE JUST SO HAPPENED to be pulling up at the same time I did.

"I was told to bring you something?" I said as I approached him.

"Mr. Riddick's sister, huh?" he asked while trying to place me.

I was like damn, I just saw you the day before and you forgot how I looked already. I could tell that it was a numbers game for him. He wasn't into getting to know people; he was only concerned about how much money he could make off them, and that was about the size of it.

"Yeah, Alonzo Riddick's sister," I informed him, and then dug inside my purse. "I've got something for you."

"Oh, yeah, the fire reports."

After I had them in hand, I gave them to him.

"Thank you," he said.

"You're welcome. So, what do you think about his case?" I got straight to the point.

"I haven't sat down and mapped out everything. But if he didn't commit the murder, then he's going to be in great shape."

"Have you decided if you're going to have a jury hearing or a judge?"

"I'm not sure, young lady. I've gotta look at the facts first. Don't worry, I'll be in touch with you and his fiancée."

"Well, if there's anything else I can do, just let me know."

"You don't oppose to testifying on his behalf, do you?" the lawyer asked.

"Of course not. I'll do anything for my brother."

"Would you lie on the stand for him?"

"No, I wouldn't lie. Why would I lie?" I was indignant.

"Just a question. What about his fiancée? Would she lie for him?"

"No, I don't think so. And why would she lie for him? Are you asking me if my brother committed that murder?"

"Did he?"

"No, he didn't. And why would you ask me that?" I replied. I was really appalled by his questioning.

"That's what I do. I ask questions."

"Well, he didn't kill those people. We paid you a lot of money, so please do your job and prove my brother's innocence," I snapped.

"Okay, I'll be in touch." He then turned around and headed into his office building. I stood there in awe, wondering why did he just try to play mind games with me? I was in disbelief about his behavior. No lawyer should express doubts to a family member of a person they are representing. That's not a code of ethics for me. Now I know he's gotta ask questions, but he sounded like he was on the federal agents' side, not Alonzo's. Were we gonna have to snatch that money back from him and find another lawyer? Or was this guy gonna put on his big-boy pants and do his fucking job?

Stressed out about my conversation with Alonzo's attorney, I climbed into my Jeep and drove back out of the parking lot. While driving down a one-way street, my phone rang and it was an unknown number. I figured that it had to be Alonzo, so I answered it.

"Hello," I said.

"Hi, my name is Juan and I was told to call you by your brother."

"What's my brother's name?" I asked him for clarity.

"Alonzo, and he was locked up in a cell at the federal building. I was cleaning the floor and he gave me your number and told me to call you."

"What did he say?"

"He told me to tell you to meet me because I have some important information to tell you."

"Are you at the federal building now?" To be clear, this guy was sounding pretty sketchy to me.

"No, I'm calling you from my cell phone."

"So you work at the federal building?" I asked.

"Yes, I mop the floors and clean the offices there. Can you meet me?"

"Where would you like to meet?" I asked.

"At the international grocery store in Norfolk on Granby Street."

"Okay. What time?"

"Now. And he said that he wanted me to tell you to bring me one thousand dollars."

"One thousand dollars?" I shouted through the phone.

"Yes, he said that Tim's gotta go."

I paused for a moment and thought about what this man was saying to me. He couldn't know Tim's name, unless Zo had mentioned it to him. But why ask for so much money? One thousand dollars was a lot of money, and that man wouldn't grab that amount of money out of thin air like that. And since I had the money on me, I agreed to meet the man at the location and time he pointed out.

Uneasy about meeting with this man I'd never met before, I drove to the international market. When I pulled into the parking lot, I searched the entire place, hoping that I would see him before he saw me. But by the time my eyes landed on him, he got out of an old pickup truck and flagged me down.

"Please don't let this man be setting me up," I said quietly to myself.

I pulled into a parking space two spaces over from where he was parked and he walked over to the driver's side of my car. I

looked at him, from head to toe, and this man was a sure home-
bred Mexican, with the appearance of a hard worker.

"You got the money?" He didn't hesitate to ask that important
question right up front.

"Yes, but tell me what my brother told you."

"He told me to tell you that Tim told the cops everything and
he needs to leave the building."

"Where was he when he told you this?"

"He was in a cell by himself. I was mopping the floor and
that's when he started talking to me."

"Does anyone else know that he told you to tell me this?"

"You mean the agents?"

"Yeah, the agents."

"Oh, no, they didn't see it when he was talking to me."

"And he told you to tell me to give you one thousand dollars?"

"Yes, and he told me to tell you to remember when you were
kids that he beat up a girl that stole ice-cream money from you."

I searched his face. "My brother told you that?" I came to the
conclusion that he couldn't have talked to no one else but my
brother. No one knew about that incident but my brother and
that little girl. Not even our parents knew about it. I knew then
that Juan wasn't lying to me, so I reached down in my purse,
counted out one thousand dollars, and handed it to him. His
face lit up like a Christmas tree.

"Thank you so much, ma'am."

"You're welcome, Juan. Just don't tell anyone that you met me
here, okay?"

"Okay," he said, and then he made his way back to his car. I
thought that he would maybe go into the grocery store and do a
little shopping, but he got into his car and hauled ass. It seemed
he wanted to get away from me as quickly as he could so that he
wouldn't have to give me back the money. But that wasn't my
call. As he put it mildly, my call was to get rid of Tim. And while
I thought about it, I knew exactly who I would get to do it.

* * *

While en route to Pricilla's house, I got a phone call from Levi. I didn't answer the first two times he called, but when he phoned the third time, I answered it. I figured he had something really important to tell me.

"What do you want?" I snapped.

"Did you see the news conference?"

"What news conference?"

"The one the federal agents had."

"No, I've been on the road. Why? What did they say?"

"They finally got someone in custody for the guy's murder out in Lake Edward."

"Did they say who?"

"No."

"So, why are you calling me?"

"Have you talked to your brother?"

"No, I haven't." Levi was on the opposing side, so I wasn't about to tell him anything.

"Word has it that he was the one that did it."

"And how did you hear that?"

"I know people."

I chuckled. "Levi, you don't know shit."

"Give it up, Alayna. I know your brother is the one that did it. I just got off the phone with the agent. She wants to see you."

Shocked by Levi's admission, I couldn't believe that he had just said that Agent McGee wanted to talk to me. I couldn't talk to her.

"Did you hear me?" he asked.

"Yeah, I heard you."

"Are you going to call her?"

"I have nothing to say to her. And since I'm your wife, you shouldn't have anything to say to her either."

"She knows about the affair you were having with Tim."

Shocked at another one of Levi's admissions, I got quiet. And Levi noticed it.

"Who told her about the affair?" he pressed the issue.

"I didn't tell her."

"Maybe Tim did when he ratted your brother out."

"How do you know that he ratted my brother out?"

"Because she told me. Right along with the fact that Alonzo is trying to put the murders of that old couple on Tim too."

"She said that?"

"Yes, she said that she has Alonzo in custody and charged him with the murder of David Cole. And while she was interviewing him, he threw Tim under the bus and told her that Tim is the one that killed that couple."

"No way. She didn't tell you that. My brother despises that lady. He would never give her any information about anything." I wanted to keep Levi as far away as possible from knowing the truth. In my eyes, he was working for the agents, and if it meant putting my brother away to get brownie points, he'd do it.

"Well, he did. And she wants you to come in and talk to her. Straighten the whole thing out with why that thirty-thousand-dollar check was really written out to you, because now she knows that you've been lying to her the whole time. Do you know that she could tie you into that murder?"

"She can't do shit, because I didn't kill those people."

"Well, she's going to press you until you tell her what you really know."

"I've gotta go," I told Levi, and then I ended his call.

He tried to call me back, but I wouldn't answer. I blocked his number altogether. And when I did that, he started calling me from his mother's number. I was forced to block her number as well.

With all the information I had now, I knew that I needed help. Alonzo was right. Tim had to go, and I knew the people that could do it.

I called Pricilla and told her that I was on my way back to her place. She told me that she saw the news conference, and I told her not to say another word over the phone; then I ended her call.

As soon as I pulled up outside her place, I called her and told her to come outside. She came out of her apartment a few minutes later.

"I need to get you to call your brother and his friend."

"And say what?"

"Tell them I need to talk to them," I added after climbing from my Jeep. "You know what, never mind. Just give me his number and I'll call him myself."

Pricilla went through her call log and called out K-Rock's cell phone number. I logged it in my phone and stuffed my phone into my pocket.

"The Feds were on TV saying that they had the person who killed that man from Lake Edward." Her face looked dreary. It looked like she had been crying from the moment I left her earlier.

"I heard. Levi called and told me that Agent McGee wanted to talk to me."

"For what?"

"I don't know."

"Well, are you going to call her?"

"Of course not. She can't help me."

"I called Zo's lawyer's office and left over a dozen messages."

"I saw him."

"Did you tell him what Levi said?"

"No, because I didn't know at the time. I just got off the phone with Levi, like literally a few minutes ago."

"Do you think Zo is capable of murdering someone?" Pricilla wanted to know.

I knew that she wanted the truth. But I also knew that she didn't want to hear it. What she wanted from me was to tell her no. Tell her no, my brother wasn't the kind of man that would go out and murder someone in cold blood. But now that I knew the truth, I was going to take it to my grave no matter the cost.

"No, he's a gentle giant. He wouldn't dare take another person's life. He prides himself with saving lives, not destroying them," I managed to say.

Pricilla embraced me. She held on to me tightly, like she didn't want to let me go. I knew that she wanted this nightmare to be over. And so did I. After she finally let me go, she stood straight up and wiped the tears from her face. "I swear, I wouldn't know what to do if I didn't have you right now."

"We're family. And family sticks together no matter what."

"If you want to find my brother, he's in Young's Park right now. Just go to the corner store off Church Street."

"Thanks," I told her, and gave her another hug.

She watched me as I climbed back into my Jeep and sped off. I knew that I was holding the cards that could set my brother free—and I was going to use them.

I didn't reach a block when my cell phone rang again. It was an unknown number, so I decided to answer it. I figured that it could be someone Alonzo told to reach out to me.

"Hello," I said softly.

"Alayna, you're just the person I want to talk to." It was Agent McGee.

My body froze solid. I couldn't believe I let her catch me with my pants down. I let this bitch catch me slipping. I wasn't supposed to answer her call.

"How did you get my number?"

"Your husband gave it to me."

"That motherfucker!" I hissed. It was barely audible. "What do you want?" I asked her.

"We need to talk."

"I have nothing to say to you."

"You're either going to meet me and talk about the real reason why your name was on that thirty-thousand-dollar check or I'm coming to arrest you."

"I already told you everything I knew."

"Well, I talked to your brother and he told me the truth. Now all I need to do is hear it from you."

"I'm not talking to you until I have a lawyer present."

"So that means that you're not going to see me tonight?" she pressed me.

"That means that I'm going to hang up with you and call my lawyer. If he says that he can accompany me when I talk to you, then you will see me tonight." I lied to her; I didn't have a fucking lawyer. But I wasn't going to tell her that.

"Well, call your lawyer and call me right back."

"Okay."

"Good, I'll be waiting," she said, and then I ended the call.

Anxiety filled my entire body at that very moment. I knew in my heart that this lady was serious. If she just threatened to come and lock me up tonight if I didn't see her, then she would make it her mission to pull in reinforcements and come looking for me.

"Damn! Damn! Damn!" I said, and started punching the steering wheel. "What am I going to do now? Alayna, you gotta think of something quick." And then it all came clear to me that I had to make shit happen now.

As far as my husband was concerned, I saw that he was on some different shit. This guy gave the Feds my fucking phone number. Was he really that fucking crazy? What was going through his mind when he decided to give that lady my number? He was really on my shit list now. There was absolutely no turning back now. It was officially over between us.

CHAPTER 34

Alonzo

THE RIDE BACK TO THE JAIL WAS LIKE A HOP, SKIP, AND A JUMP. THE quicker I was there, the quicker the COs had me back en route to my cell block. The Black correctional officer escorting me couldn't wait to get me in the hallway so he could run his mouth.

"So, is it true?" he asked.

"Is what true?" I questioned him, but I already knew what this was about.

"They got you on new murder charges?"

"Nah, that wasn't me."

"Well, they charged you with it," he said.

"It's just preliminary. I'll prove my innocence in court."

"I heard they had you on the robbery too."

"I didn't do that either. I wasn't there the night that man was killed."

"Is it true that you're a firefighter?"

"Yeah, I was."

"They're saying that you defrauded a lot of old people."

"I didn't do it alone."

"So you're in a ring?" he asked.

"If that's what you want to call it."

"They should put you on that *American Greed* show. I know that shit would be interesting."

"I'm sure it would be too."

"So, how much did you make?"

"I can't say," I lied. I wasn't about to tell this random-ass narc how much money I made off that insurance scam. Was he crazy?

"How long did you do it?"

"Can't say."

"Was it one year? Two? Six months?"

"Can't say."

"Got a lawyer?"

"Yeah, I got a lawyer."

"Well, he better be good, because you're going to need a helluva defense."

"Don't worry, I've got one."

When we approached my cell block, he called out to the other CO to open the sliding cell door. "Open Door B!" he shouted, and then the door opened.

I stepped on the opposite side of the bar and waited for the door to close before the CO in the booth would open the other door to the cell block. After I was cleared, the door finally opened and I walked through. All eyes were on me as I walked into my cell.

My cellmate, Wayne, greeted me as soon as I walked into the cell.

"You a'ight?" he asked.

"Yeah, I'm good. Why?"

"Because everybody is talking about the Feds snatching you up while you were having a visit earlier."

"Who told you that?"

"Nobody. But everybody is talking about it. You're in jail. Word gets around real fast."

"So ain't nobody said anything to you?"

"Nah, I'm just hearing certain niggas around here talking about it. So I heard you were a firefighter."

"Yeah, I was," I said as I sat down on my bunk bed.

"Have you ever almost lost your life in duty?"

"Yeah, a couple of times."

"Have you ever tried to save someone and they died before you could save them?"

"Yeah."

"Did that fuck you up? I mean, your head and all?" Wayne asked.

"Yeah, that happened from time to time."

"I don't think I could do that type of work. I'm a selfish dude, so I ain't putting my life on the line for someone else's."

"I used to think that same way."

"Was they talking about you on the news?"

"What did they say?"

"They said that they got someone in custody that killed the old man in Lake Edward. The Feds and the man's family was talking to the newspeople earlier. They had like a conference or something."

"Well, I ain't killed nobody, so, no, they weren't talking about me."

"That ain't what everybody else is saying."

"Don't believe everything you hear, kid."

"I try not to. You married?"

"Nope."

"Got kids?"

"Nope."

"That's good, because you don't want your kids hearing bad shit about you. That could fuck them up. Then kids and shit in school would tease them. And before you know it, your kids can't take it anymore. Bring a gun to school and try to kill every-body that bullied them. That shit is real."

"Yes, it is. Do you have kids, Wayne?"

"Nah, but my girl is pregnant. She's like five months, I think."

I chuckled. "You don't know how far along she is?"

"Every day it changes. I'm just trying to get out of here, old head. This place ain't for me."

"This place ain't for anyone."

"I'm with you," Wayne agreed.

"Think you've got a good chance in getting out of here before your child is born?"

"Hopefully. But the white folks love packing niggas up in jail. They get paid a lot of money for each body they keep locked up. They charge us for being in here on a daily basis and then the government pays them too. Keeping niggas locked up is big business. It's gotten so bad, the judge will give you ten years just for beating your girlfriend up. Ten years for possession of one hundred dollars of dope. And life for murder. It's insane."

"Well, if you get the chance to get out of here, change your life. Be an example for your baby," I advised.

"You ain't gotta tell me that shit twice. I've already made up my mind that I'm changing my life. The niggas in here are petty and they'll stab you for little or nothing. It's a jungle in this bitch."

"Have you had any fights since you've been in here?"

"I try to avoid those. You see I'm like the smallest guy in here."

I chuckled because he was right. He was a small-framed guy.

"Chow!" I heard a male correctional officer shout.

"Dinner's calling," he commented, and slid off his top bunk. But when he saw that I hadn't budged, he stopped in his tracks. "You're not hungry?" he asked.

"Nah, I'm good."

"Well, get your tray and hand it to me."

"Just tell them I told you to give it to you."

"That's not how it works around here. You're gonna have to physically grab the tray from them."

I stood up and followed him out to the cell block floor. As soon as the CO passed me the food tray, I handed it to my cell-mate. He thanked me and followed me back into the cell. "I sure appreciate this. You see they feed us like we're ten years old."

I looked at both trays and he was right. What was given to us was merely peanuts. Who could live off one sandwich, one scoop of mashed potatoes, and one scoop of green beans? Not me. And certainly not him. He definitely showed me his appreciation as he piled everything on the same tray and danced around with his arms in a cheerful fashion. I watched him with every spoonful of food he pushed into his mouth and he was happy.

"Tell me who I need to watch out for?" I asked him, loud enough so that only he could hear me.

He pointed to a white guy who looked like he was part of the Aryan Nation, with tattoos all over his face, neck, arms, and chest. "That's Preecher. He thinks he runs shit around here. He's got two other guys that he's taken underneath his wing. They'll do anything he asks them to do."

"What about that tall guy with the Afro pick in his head?" I asked him.

"Frank? Oh, yeah, he's an asshole. Between him and the Aryan Brother, they think they run the block."

"Does the Black guy with the pick hang out with that crew of guys sitting at the table with him?"

"Yeah, they watch each other's back. I stay clear of all them. They're bad news."

"Have they had words with one another?"

"Yeah, once, since I've been here, but the old head Tommy that has the cell at the far end of the block stopped them before the shit hit the fan. He's like the peacemaker."

"Is Tommy out there now?"

"Nah, he's probably in his cell. But he's the old man with the gray dreadlocks. He let them grow all the way past his ass. Everybody in here respects him."

"They're gonna respect me too," I acknowledged.

"Stand your ground and they will."

"How are the COs that walk this block?"

"They a'ight, I guess. But that doesn't mean try to be their friend. They are the po-po, so they're gonna do their job at the end of the day."

"Duly noted."

CHAPTER 35

Tim

I WAS SHOCKED THAT ALAYNA PICKED UP THE PHONE AND CALLED ME. She must have thought about the severity in my voice when I told her that I would ruin her if my wife found out about Jesse. She didn't have her big brother, Alonzo, out there to protect her anymore.

"How can I help you?" I asked.

"We need to talk."

"There's nothing to talk about."

"Yes, there is, Tim. And I've got to get this off my chest."

"So do it."

"I need to say it to you, face-to-face."

"You know I can't leave the station."

"But this is important."

"Is it about you sneaking into Alonzo's office?"

"Yes, and I want to talk about us too. I've been trying to get you out of my head, but I can't. I wanna see if we can work this out."

"But there's nothing to work out. Your brother committed those murders, and I'm getting as far away as I can from him and that situation."

"Tim, will you please see me? Just one more time? If we can't get by this, then I won't ever call you again."

"Come up here."

"You know how that'll look. Meet me somewhere," she countered.

"Where?"

"At the old salvage junkyard twenty miles away from the station," she suggested. "Can you meet me there now?"

"Yes, I can," I agreed.

On my way out of the station, I brushed by Jesse. He wanted to know where I was going.

"I've got an errand to run," I told him.

"But what if we get an emergency call?"

"You and Paul can handle it."

"This is not like you. Tell me what's going on!"

"I'm going to iron some things out."

"With who?"

"Alayna."

"I fucking knew it. You act like you can't let her go."

"Don't get your panties up in a bunch. She called to talk to me. I didn't call her."

"And what could she possibly have to say to you?"

"I'm going to go and find out."

"You be careful, because I don't trust her."

"I'm only doing it because she threatened to tell Kirsten about us."

"I fucking knew it. She's a manipulating cunt."

"I'm gonna handle it. Don't you worry."

"What if she tells your wife anyway?"

"After tonight, she won't, believe me."

"I hope you're right."

"I am. Just sit by your phone, and if I need anything, I'll call you."

"Okay."

En route to the old salvage yard, I made a quick beeline to my house. I had to use the bathroom really bad. I knew when Kirsten saw me, she would want to know why I had come home.

When I entered the house, she was front and center in front of the TV. "You are going to live a long time," she said.

"So they say," I commented, and chuckled.

"I saw the news conference," she added.

"I did too."

"Did the Feds call you?"

"They stopped by my office. I was going to call you, but we'd been hit really hard with work down at the station, and it just kept slipping my mind."

"What did they say? Was Alonzo the one that killed that man from Lake Edward?"

"Yes, he was."

"Oh, man, I was hoping you'd say that he didn't. What's gotten into that man? I allowed him to be around our son." Kirsten sounded disappointed.

"I don't know. But it'll all come out in court."

"Are you sure you didn't know anything about it?"

"No, honey, I didn't. But I did have my suspicions."

"You don't think those federal agents are going to implicate you in all that nonsense, do you?"

"No, honey, they're not."

"I hope not, because we would be the talk of the town. Just imagine what our friends would say? The kids would get eaten alive at school. It would be a shit show for sure."

"Stop stressing yourself out. We're gonna be fine. We won't get any of that backlash."

"So, what did the federal agents say?"

"They said that they have a witness that could put Alonzo at the scene on the night the old man was murdered."

"Oh, my God! That's so horrible. And to think that we let him attend our children's Bar Mitzvahs."

"You never know a person until their secrets are revealed."

"Think he has a lawyer?"

"If he doesn't, he better get one now."

"Oh, that's such a shame."

"I'll talk to you when I come out of the bathroom," I told Kirsten, and broke away from our conversation. If I allowed it, she'd talk me to death and I'd forget all about why I came home in the first place.

"Is that why you came home?" she commented.

"Yes," I shouted as I headed toward the bathroom.

While I sat down on the toilet, I wondered what Alayna was going to say to me. There really wasn't anything I wanted to hear from her, other than she knew that her brother killed those people and that she was going to come to my side. Other than that, I didn't wanna hear shit that she had to say.

It only took me a few minutes to take a crap. After I stood up and washed my hands, I exited the bathroom and walked back through the living room so that I could leave the house. But, of course, Kirsten found a way to stop me again.

"Do you think that Alayna knew about this all along?"

"I can't say."

"Well, I think she did. As a matter of fact, I hope she had something to do with it, so they can haul her ass off to jail too. She's not innocent, you know. It wouldn't surprise me if she was there."

I looked at my wife like she was crazy. I knew for a fact that Alayna wasn't there when Alonzo committed that murder. Any of the murders, for that matter. But Kirsten already had it out for Alayna; so in her eyes, she wanted her to be guilty. If she could lock Alayna up herself and throw away the key, she would. She'd do anything to get rid of her.

"I'm sure the federal agents will figure that one out."

"On TV, they said that there might be others that helped commit the murder. So I'm sold on the idea that she could've been that other person."

"Kirsten, she was at the station with me when the murders were committed."

"Oh, I forgot, you're gonna take up for your girlfriend. She can do no wrong in your eyes." Kirsten became visibly upset.

"I'm not taking up for her, honey. I'm only giving you the facts."

"Don't worry. It'll all come out in the end."

"Yes, it will, honey. Yes, it will," I said, and then I made my exit.

"You be careful out there," I heard her shout from the inside of the house. But I ignored her. I figured that she wouldn't hear me anyway, so why bother to respond?

Ten minutes into the drive, Jesse rang my cell phone. I answered it on the first ring. "Hello."

"Are you with her yet?"

"No, I am not."

"Why is it taking you so long to get there?"

"Because I had to stop off at home first."

"Is everything all right there?"

"Yes, Jesse, it is."

"Well, be careful."

"I will. Now don't call me back. I will call you," I said abruptly, and then I ended the call. I mean, what was wrong with this guy? Was he crazy or something? I saw, right now, I'm gonna have to end things with him.

CHAPTER 36

Alayna

WHEN I ASKED TIM FOR THIS MEETING, I KNEW THAT THIS WOULD be the ideal place to meet, because it was away from the road. We would be in the woods—literally, the backwoods—behind a metal salvage junkyard. He didn't know it, but I came prepared, because I knew he was trying to set me up so that he could save his own ass. So, with him out of the way, Alonzo could definitely beat the murder rap and come home to his family.

I watched him as he got out of his car. And when he got to the edge of his hood, I climbed out of my Jeep and met him halfway. Even though it was night out, I could still see his smile.

"Tell me what you want," he started off saying after he leaned his body against the hood of his car.

"I want to talk about us," I said as I approached him.

"There is no 'us' anymore. You made that perfectly known when you left the station earlier."

"Well, I wanna talk about my brother and our relationship."

"Which one you wanna talk about first?" he was curious to know.

"Let's talk about my brother."

"I'm listening."

"Tim, you've known him for a long time, you know he didn't do those things the Feds said that he did."

"Correction, I *thought* I knew your brother. Let's face it, Alayna, he has changed. I know for a fact that he had something to do with that couple getting murdered. I believe that he murdered them. Just like I believe that he murdered that old man in Lake Edward. Remember I came to you about that the night I saw it on the news?"

"No, I don't remember that."

"Alayna, yes, you do. When I saw it, I ran to your room and asked you about it, and you laughed at me. But you know he did that. And you know he stole that man's money from his safe too. So just admit it," he pointed out. "Check it out. I spoke with the Feds and they said that if we testify against him, we could get off without doing any federal time. So, whatcha say? This is a deal of a lifetime."

"So you've been talking to the agents since the last time we spoke?"

"Do you know how much shit I've got to lose? I'm not taking the fall for your hothead-ass brother. He killed those people and he took their money, and I'm going to save my own ass, and if you pass up the chance to do the same, then you're even dumber than I thought you were." He was scolding me.

"I knew you were a piece of shit, you fucking rat!" I roared. "Get 'em!" I shouted, and the two dudes I ordered to hit Tim came from behind his car, aimed their guns at him, and started spraying him. *POP! POP! POP! POP! POP! POP! POP!* Seven shots penetrated the rat, and all he could do was try to shield himself with his arms. But that didn't help.

I stood there and watched him as he took his last breath. "Fucking traitor!" I shouted at him, and then I spit where he lay.

"Take his wallet so it'll look like a robbery."

"Got it," one of the guys said.

"Oh, and check and see if he has a wire on him," I ordered them.

I continued to stand there as one of them searched his pockets.

"Yeah, I found a recorder," the same masked man said.

"Is it on?"

"Yep."

"Take the tape out. And throw it to me. Take the recorder and get rid of it."

After the guy threw me the tape, I slid it down inside my panties and then I watched as both guys fled on foot. I waited five minutes and then I rushed back to my Jeep, grabbed my cell phone, and dialed 911. I knew I had to put on an act. Make it look like we were ambushed, if I wanted to get out of this.

"Here goes nothing," I said, and then I put the call on speakerphone.

"You're calling 911. What's your emergency?"

"I'm standing out here with my ex-lover and two guys came from out of nowhere and killed him. Please send the police now!" I screamed.

"You're saying he's dead?"

"Yes, he's dead. They shot him a lot of times. Please send the police now before they come back."

"Ma'am, are you hurt in any way?"

"No."

"Okay, then tell me what is your name?"

"Alayna Curry."

"And where are you, Alayna?"

"I'm over here at BJ's metal salvage junkyard, off Military Highway."

"Stay there and I'm sending help now."

"Please hurry," I told her, and then I smiled in a wicked fashion, knowing that now that Tim was gone, my brother had a chance to beat his murder charges.

But I knew that I wasn't done there. The operator told me to stay on the phone until the cops arrived, but I ignored her instructions and ended the call. I knew that I needed to get Pricilla on the phone. I needed an alibi from her, just so that I could cover my own ass.

I called her and she answered on the second ring. I tried to sound as distraught as I could. I needed to make it believable.

"Pricilla, you're not going to believe it!" I screamed through the phone.

"What happened?" She seemed alarmed.

"Someone just murdered Tim. He's lying right here on the ground, shot dead!" I yelled.

"Did you see who did it?" she shouted back. "Are you sure he's dead?"

"Two guys showed up out of nowhere and robbed Tim. He tried to fight them off, but he couldn't overpower them and they shot him."

"Call the police. He might still be alive."

"I did."

"Where are you?"

"Somewhere in the woods. Near a salvage yard."

"Are you alone?"

"Yes, I am scared that they will come back."

"Well, get the 911 operator back on the phone and they'll stay on the phone with you until the cops get there."

"Okay," I said, and ended our call.

I called the operator right back, but I could hear the police and ambulance in the distance among the trees and the old wreckage. While I was calling the 911 operator back, she was beating in on the other line, so I answered it.

"Ma'am, I told you to stay on the line."

"I know, but I had to call someone. I was afraid." I continued to sound like I was in despair.

"Well, the paramedics and the police should be pulling up at any second now."

"I hear them coming now."

"Well, stay on the phone until they get there and then I'll turn you over to them."

"Okay," I said, and then I fell silent. I tried my hardest to sound like I was alone and afraid, because I knew that my call was being recorded. And I knew that when Agent McGee finally got to listen to it, she was going to pick it apart.

"They're here now," I told the dispatcher.

"Okay, then I'm gonna turn over the call to them," she said, and disconnected the call.

Both paramedics tried everything in their power to revive

Tim, but I knew he was dead, and they knew it too. Now I had to put on a show for the cops, because I knew that they were going to come full throttle.

They were both white men and they had a ton of questions for me.

"Are you okay, ma'am?" one officer started off.

"No, I'm not. I just witnessed my ex-lover get robbed and killed."

"What is your name?"

"Alayna Curry."

"And who is the deceased man?" the same cop asked me.

"Tim Stancil."

"So you said that he's your ex-lover?"

"Yes!" I continued to cry. I even buried my face inside my hands a couple of times during his questioning.

"So, are you both married?"

"Yes."

"So take us back to what happened?" the cop asked me to explain.

"Well, I called him and told him that we needed to discuss our arrangement, so we decided to meet out here."

"Why out here? You guys were in the middle of nowhere."

"Because he didn't want his wife to see us."

"Okay, so continue."

"Well, when we got out of our vehicles, we talked for a bit about our relationship, and then out of nowhere, two guys show up. They cornered him and I tried to run. But one of the guys aimed his gun at me and stopped me and told me that if I ran, he was going to kill both of us. So I stood still and watched them as they robbed him."

"And what happened next?"

"Well, I thought Tim was just going to give them his valuables and they would leave, but he decided that he wanted to play hero and tried to take the gun from one of the guys. He was wrestling with the guy and then I heard a gunshot. And when Tim fell to the ground, the guys ran off."

"So they never tried to rob you?"

"I think they wanted to, but Tim stopped them from doing it because of what transpired with him."

"Did you touch Tim after he hit the ground?"

"No, I was scared and hopped back into my Jeep."

"At any point, did you want to leave?" the same cop continued.

"Yes, I did. But when I seen a car taillight leaving from the other side of the trees, I figured that they had left and that I was no longer in danger."

"Did anyone know that you were coming out here to meet him?"

"No, but right before you pulled up, I called my brother's fiancée and told her what happened."

"Where do you work?" he questioned next.

"I used to work as a firefighter."

"What do you mean that you *were* a firefighter?"

"I quit my job the other day."

"Is that where the deceased also worked?"

"Yes." My cries kept coming. I swear, I could get an Academy Award after all of this.

"Which city?"

"Virginia Beach. We worked in the Haygood district."

Both cops looked at each other. "You wouldn't be talking about the station where one of the firefighters was arrested for murder?"

"Yep, that's the one."

"Stand right there. We'll be right back," the cop said, and then he and his partner stepped away from me. I knew they suspected foul play, so I knew that I needed to turn it up a notch.

"Can I call my husband?" I yelled.

"No, not yet. Just stay put," he instructed me. So I leaned against my Jeep and covered my face with my hands. I let out the floodgates then, because these cops were going to be watching me like a hawk and I had to play the role. If I didn't, I was going to jail for life too.

Finally, after sitting around and talking to the two male homicide detectives for over an hour, they let me go. I was a little fraz-

zled, trying to get my story straight, but I ended up pulling it together toward the end. I felt even better after I was allowed to
leave. Without hesitation, I hauled ass out of there.

I knew I couldn't go home, so I went to Pricilla's apartment.
When she opened the door, I could tell that she was shocked to
see me.

"Is everything all right?" she asked as she stood in the doorway.

"Tim's dead," I said with finality.

Pricilla gave me a look of pure horror. She looked over my
shoulders and into the street behind me. And then she peered
out the door, from the left to the right side of me. After she saw
that the coast was clear, she grabbed me by the hand and said,
"Come in here before someone sees you."

Inside the apartment, she led me to the sofa. "So tell me what
happened."

I sat there and thought for a moment about which story I
should tell her. Because if I told her the truth, she'd probably
have a nervous breakdown and would end up testifying against
me, her brother, and his friend at the trial. So I decided to do
the next best thing, and that was to give her the same story I
gave the detectives, because I was trying to stay out of jail and
bring my brother home in the process.

And I knew right then and there, if I had to burn my friends,
my colleagues—and my honesty with them all—to save my
brother, I would without a moment's hesitation. I would set that
blaze.

4·23